WHO KILLED NUTTY NUCKLEBALL?

Other Books by Jerry Rannow

"WRITING TELEVISON COMEDY"

"SURVIVING HOLLYWOOD"

"THIS ONE'LL KILLYA"
(A Springer McKay Novel)

"DIE LAUGHING"
(A Springer McKay Novel)

"THE BROADWAY COMEDY MURDERS"
(A Springer McKay Novel)

Available at AMAZON.COM
WEBSITE: www.jerryrannow.com

WHO KILLED NUTTY NUCKLEBALL?

Jerry Rannow

Copyright © 2019 by Jerry Rannow.
Cover Design by Ron Schulz.
Author photo by Mick Luvin Photography

Library of Congress Control Number:		2019906780
ISBN:	Hardcover	978-1-7960-3864-4
	Softcover	978-1-7960-3865-1
	eBook	978-1-7960-3877-4

All rights reserved. No part of this book may be reproduced or transmitted in any form or by any means, electronic or mechanical, including photocopying, recording, or by any information storage and retrieval system, without permission in writing from the copyright owner.

This is a work of fiction. Names, characters, places and incidents either are the product of the author's imagination or are used fictitiously, and any resemblance to any actual persons, living or dead, events, or locales is entirely coincidental.

Print information available on the last page.

Rev. date: 06/12/2019

To order additional copies of this book, contact:
Xlibris
1-888-795-4274
www.Xlibris.com
Orders@Xlibris.com
795643

Dedicated To

The TOPPS Bubblegum Company

CHAPTER ONE

I scrambled through the thorny woods—a bloodthirsty mob in pursuit!

A bullet parted my hair!

An arrow parted the part!

I skidded to a *stop*, surrounded by yappy dogs with drippy fangs.

Thinking quickly I sang, *"How Much is That Doggy in the Window,"* accompanied by a chorus of howls.

I continued to run for my life.

Glancing back I saw the angry mob charging past the dogs who had segued into their rendition of *"You Ain't Nothin' But A Hound Dog."*

If you're wondering how I got myself into this mess, here's how it all began.

I was in my office at Warner Brothers, the day the network canceled *"Heaven Help Us,"* a sitcom I was writing about madcap monks in a monastery. This left me with no choice but to load up on free office supplies and face a world where I bear the mark of failure.

I headed Wolfgang, my '85 Beemer, over to Cantor's Deli on Fairfax to commiserate over lunch with Leo Merkin, who had yet to show up. My old college bud has a gift for tardiness. One time I arrived an hour late to teach him a lesson. He arrived an hour later.

An hour later there was Leo, his mouth twisted in an offline grin due to online dentures. Spindly legs supported a substantial gut overseen by a melon-like head. A cross between Tweedledee and Tweedledum.

Leo and I had a comedy act in school. Headlined all the talent shows. Me, the straight man. Leo, the stooge, born to take a pie in the face.

"Springer old pal," he announced, "this is your lucky day."

I knew what Leo was up to. "Don't tell me," I said, "this is another one of your hair-brained schemes."

"It's baseball," he beamed. "Minor league baseball. Huge growth industry. Bought the *Clowns* for a song."

"You bought clowns...?"

"It's a team in Wisconsin."

"Uh-huh," I nodded. "Why are they called clowns?"

Leo shrugged. "I don't know, but they sure sound like fun."

"Where'd you get the money to buy a baseball team?"

"You won't believe it."

"I'll believe it."

"I won the lottery!"

"I don't believe it."

"Me neither," he said. "I made a mistake on my birth date and won big until the taxes were sucked out, but it's still a tidy sum. So, what do ya say, you'll be my general manager, wear a uniform, sit on the bench, be one of the boys. You've always been a baseball nut. All through school you smelled like bubble gum."

True, but I had to ask, "Don't you have to have experience to run a baseball team?"

"Hey, money trumps experience any time," he assured me. "So are you ready to play ball?"

I was intrigued, but hesitant to follow another one of Leo's enterprises. Last time, we got stuck with sixteen herds of sheep in a depressed sheep market...Then again, baseball beats the hell out of sheep.

"What's it pay?" I asked.

"Think of a number."

"Six-hundred and fifty-four million."

Leo laughed so hard he slipped out of the booth. Re-arranging himself, he said, "You and your whimsy, cracks me up."

"What's it pay?" I repeated.

"Same as the players," he said. "Two-hundred a month."

"That's not a living wage."

Leo's lips jutted to a pout…"Geez, Springer, I'm only trying to recapture your boyhood dream."

Leo Merkin always manages to suck me into his nonsense. There's something about this goof that activates my caregiver gene and, what the hey, a comedy writer like me will fit right in with a bunch of clowns.

CHAPTER TWO

Armed with absolutely no knowledge of what I was getting myself into, I fired-up Wolfgang and we headed east out of L.A., through Vegas, Utah, across Wyoming, Nebraska, into Iowa, Illinois, and up to Wisconsin.

Leo chose to fly. He's afraid of driving.

A few hours after entering the majesty of Wisconsin's Northwoods Wolfgang fell into a coma and was escorted by Clowntown Auto Repair— *"Use us and you'll never go anywhere again."*

We were towed through Clowntown's main drag—four taverns, three gun stores, two taxidermists and a nail salon.

I deposited Wolfgang at Clownfelder's Garage, grabbed my duffel and headed across the street to Clownhowser's Bed & Barn, featuring indoor plumbing, air-cooling fans, valet horse parking out back.

Three-hundred pounds of Spike Clownhowser overwhelmed the hotel desk. He eyed me warily. "You ain't from around here, are ya?"

"Nope," I answered. "California."

"You one'a them commies?"

"Not that I recall."

It was impossible not to notice Clownhowser had one arm and no left ear. He wore a pistol on each hip, an ammunition belt slung across his chest, a shotgun cradled in his lap.

"Expecting a war?" I casually remarked.

"Enforcin' my amended rights," Clownhowser firmly stated. "Man can't be too careful with wild animals and humans and such... You here for the shootdown?"

"What shootdown is that?"

"The Annual Clowntown Shootdown," he said. "After church on Sunday the man who shoots the most wildlife wins a statue of a beaver."

Clownhowser's splotchy eyes went slitty…"I'm gonna get me some wolfs," he rumbled. "Attacked me once. Whole pack. Wolfs are Satan's soldiers."

He heaved up from behind the desk, swung the stump of is left leg into my unsuspecting hand. "Them wolfs was havin' me for supper," he seethed. "Be a goner if my ex-wife hadn't scared 'em off to protect her alimony."

Clownhowser snatched back his stump. "So, stranger, what brings you to our neck'a the woods?"

"I'm with the baseball team. Y'know, the *Clowns*…?"

"What'cha wanna do that for?"

"I'm the new general manager."

"Not for long. Last one got run out'a town."

My room at the Bed & Barn smelled like barn. Knotsy-piney eyes stared at me. The rabbit ears only get Fox News.

Using my knees for a desk, I jotted a few notes for the book I plan to get out of this experience. As usual, I'll see life with a crack in it. Reality can always use a few laughs.

CHAPTER THREE

I decided to hike over to the ballpark, got lost, asked a farmer for directions. "Head down to Clown Acres," he pointed, "past Clown Creek, over to Clown Swamp, then a right on Broadway, a left on Hollywood Boulevard, but you don't wanna go there, people don't go there no more. Sure the team was a winner way back when, but now they lose a lot more than they win and nobody gives a shit."

I entered Clown Memorial Stadium, a relic from days gone by. Holds several hundred fans who sit in seats that are either broken or missing. The hand-operated scoreboard leans to the left and, if you don't count the gopher holes, the diamond's still in pretty bad shape.

The dilapidated outfield wall was awash with faded advertising. Ty Cobb hawking men's garters. Ted Williams urging us to smoke Camels. Jackie Robinson touting the glories of Wonder Bread.

Leo Merkin tripped out of the dugout, trotted over and handed me a baseball cap adorned with the face of a clown. More grim than Bozoish. His eyes follow you.

"Like the new *Clown* logo?" Leo asked. "I designed it myself."

"He looks mentally disturbed," I said.

"It's the sad face behind the happy clown."

"Give him a knife and he'll stab teenagers."

Leo broke up. "Humor! Love it! And wait till you see our uniforms. They're getting patched up, but we'll have 'em by game time...Did you hear what I said? *Game Time!* We are about to ride a wave of glory!"

"And me without my noodle."

"My fondest dream has always been to own a baseball team."

"You told me your fondest dream is to be a train engineer at Disneyworld."

"That too," Leo granted. "Oh, and before I forget I went over to the barbershop to get my nostrils clipped and the barber told me Clowntown was named after the first settler, Mongrel J. Clown, who was an atheist fleeing religious persecution. There's a long line of Clowns to this day. Mayor Mongrel J. Clown, a direct descendant, is the muckiest-muck. Owns the First Clown Security Integrity Fidelity Bank & Trust Company which owns the whole town."

Leo threw a brotherly arm around me. "Welcome to my ballpark, partner. Let me show you around."

Leo ushered me into the *Clown* dugout. Spit soaked my sneakers.

We made our way through a dark passage to the players' clubhouse.

George Washington Played Here was scrawled across the concrete wall.

The clubhouse featured a dirt floor and the whiff of lingering farts. A lone bulb illuminated an empty water cooler containing the skeletal remains of a goldfish. Cracked wooden benches lined severely damaged lockers. A single shower was out of order. Half the toilet seat was missing.

"What do you think?" Leo asked.

"I like what you've done with the place."

Back on the field we climbed a rickety stairway to a small second level press box which was to be my office.

My foot punched a hole in the floor.

"The ballpark needs a little work," said Leo.

"The ballpark needs a new ballpark," I said, freeing my leg from the hole.

"That's exactly what I plan to do," said Leo as he gazed down at the field. "I'll re-do the whole stadium. A multipurpose venue. VIP suites, retractable roof, racing beer cans, Bruce Springsteen, the Rolling Stones...!"

"Okay, okay, Leo," I interrupted, "before you book The Mormon Tabernacle Choir, exactly how much money did you win?"

He shook his head. "Sorry, can't tell you. Money makes me mysterious and I've never been mysterious before, so that's what I'm gonna be, mysterious." He nudged me with his elbow and missed. "C'mon, Springer, have I ever steered you wrong?"

The answer was a resounding yes, but I couldn't bring myself to shoot down Leo's enthusiasm. If my friend can afford to be mysterious the idea of a new ballpark sounds great.

"Okay," I pitched in, "first, we have to work on improving our team. Nobody pays to see a loser."

"Not to worry," Leo assured me. "I hired a new manager."

"I thought hiring was my job."

"Saved you the trouble. Ever hear of Heinie Pratt?"

"Who hasn't? The man's a legend."

"Like Babe Ruth."

"I always wondered why Pratt's not in the Hall of Fame?"

"Let's find out," said Leo. "He's meeting us for drinks."

CHAPTER FOUR

Clownhowser's Bed & Barn boasted a cheesy little watering hole called the Big Rack Lounge. Patrons displayed a colossal variety of weaponry. A mounted moose head seemed to say, "Next time I get the gun."

Spike Clownhowser tended bar, using his shotgun as a crutch. He sported a shoulder-holstered handgun.

"German Luger," I observed. "A classic."

"Best online," he solidly stated. "Toggle-locked recoil-operated semi-automatic. Hitler's personal favorite."

He whipped out the Lugar, waved it at Leo and shouted—"Achtung!" Leo's hands shot up in surrender.

Clownhowser snarked a laugh, pointed the Lugar at me and said, "What'll ya have? I recommend the rusty nail."

I ordered a rusty nail.

I hate rusty nails.

Leo turned to me, saying, "Jiminy creepers, Springer, check out this place, it's like the Old West."

"Yeah," I agreed, "time travel really works."

A wad of phlegm flew past my nose, landing in an ashtray. The source of the phlegm was a jug-eared head featuring a megawatt nose and thick lenses in heavy black frames. Bald, beefier than his playing days, there was no mistaking the imposing presence of Heinie Pratt.

In a clipped, crusty voice he roared—*"Barkeep! Moonshine! Leave the jar!"*

Leo was mired in awe and unable to speak, so I introduced myself, adding, "It's a pleasure to have you aboard, Mister Pratt."

"At my age you gotta make yourself useful," he grumbled.

An attractive young waitress passed by. Heinie grabbed her around the waist, looked deeply into her eyes and asked, "How'd you like to see the biggest dick in baseball?"

The waitress slapped him hard across the face and hurried off, leaving Heinie muttering, "It worked better when I was a player, but everything worked better when I was a player."

He pointed a gnarly finger at Leo. "Who's this twerp?"

Leo came to life. "Oh, me...? I'm the, uh, owner."

"I *hate* owners," Heinie puffed through his shaggy moustache. "A bunch'a thiefs and rapscallions!"

Leo had no ready reply, so I said, "Mister Pratt, I want you to know we're thrilled and excited to have a legend like you managing our *Clowns*."

"*Clowns*, huh?" snuffed Heinie. "Back in the old days we had the *Indianapolis Clowns*, formerly the *Ethiopian Clowns* who had to close down cuz there's no baseball in Ethiopia, but Woody, Peanuts, Choo-Choo you never heard of, but you heard of Henry Aaron, so what the hell am I doin' in this fuckwater town?"

"Well, to begin with," I tactfully explained, "our team hasn't been living up to expectations."

"They stink like socks," said Leo.

"And they need your leadership," I quickly added.

"I'll tell ya about leadership," Heinie bellowed. "Leadership is a swift kick in the nuts, ain't like the old days when boys were men and men were men, and if they weren't they kept their pants zipped."

"I'm sure they did," I acknowledged. "But most of our players are boys, still growing up, on their own for the first time. They need care and guidance."

Heinie sucked a chug of moon, wiped his mouth on the frayed sleeve of his plaid sports jacket and declaimed—"Boys are kids and kids today are *soft*, a bunch'a thumb suckers, mollycoddled mugwumps, no get up and go like the get up that got up and went cuz their noses are glued to those devices suckin' the soul from these United States, fuck that shit, gimme Bell Telephone every time."

He nodded for me to agree.

"I think I see your point."

Heinie rambled on. "The hardest thing in baseball is to play baseball, which is what it's all about, and you never know what's goin' on, and why it's so tough for a smart person, gotta teach 'em the right way to play the game cuz the devil's in the details, losers burn in hell, so let's get out there and hang our heads high!"

In the midst of puzzling together Heinie's exclusive language, I felt a hefty slap on my back, turned to see a pale fortyish face smattered with acne. He sported a pretentious ponytail, camouflage business suit and matching ammunition vest.

"It is indeed a very very great honor for me to meet the tremendous men who will lead my fantastic *Clowns* to victory," he twanged through his nose.

He introduced himself as Mayor Mongrel J. Clown, who comes from a very very long line of Clowns and is, in fact, a pure-blooded descendant of Clowntown's founding father, the beloved Mongrel J. Clown.

We introduced ourselves as ourselves, except for Heinie who glared at the Mayor and snarled, "Politician, huh…?"

"Yes," replied the Mayor, "I was destined for a political career. My playpen had a podium." He emitted a snort.

"I *hate* politicians," Heinie thundered. "A bunch'a dicksuckin' monkeycocks."

Mayor Clown forced an insincere laugh and said, "I like a man who speaks his mind. Although I should warn you I will be umpiring all of your home games. As a matter of fact, I will be the *only* umpire on the field. All of my decisions will be *final!*"

Heinie mooshed nose-to-nose with Mayor Clown and seethed—"I ain't trustin' any sombitch like you with no jaw and empty eyes."

Mayor Clown remembered a dental appointment and scurried off.

Heinie threw back his moonshine, slammed the jar on the bar and said…"I gotta get me a gun."

CHAPTER FIVE

Leo slid a contract under my door. It states that I am now employed by the *Clowntown Clowns* of the *Northern Walleye League* which is *NOT* affiliated with any Major or Minor League.

In other words, bottom of the boonies.

The *Clowns are* the perennial cellar-dwellers in a league that consists of *the Beaverbrook Bullheads, Timberville Splinters, Dead Lake Loons, West Sweden Sturgeons, Scum River Cavaliers, Musty Valley Flying Squirrels*, and the dreaded *Kickapoo Hayhaulers*.

The schedule calls for sixty games, July first to the end of August. We're mid-way through the season and the *Clowns* are in last place with a record of 9 wins and 21 losses.

They do occupy first place in bench-clearing brawls.

We have a roster of only eleven players. Most teams have at least twenty, so we're barely equipped to compete leaving me to wonder if I'm firmly planted on quicksand.

…But I can't walk out on Leo. He's the one who brought me out of my shell. At parties I would sit in a corner mumbling witty remarks. Leo would hear me and fall on the floor laughing, causing the others to ask—"*What did Springer say?*" So, I repeated my witty to total silence. It lacked spontaneity, laid a mortified egg. But Leo came to my rescue. Urged me to speak up. To be fearless. To "*dare to sound stupid,*" which I have done ever since with great success.

Resplendent in my prison-gray uniform, I watched the *Clowns* take batting and fielding practice. Long hair. Beards. A collection of Neanderthal wanna-bees.

A coach was advising a hitter, "Don't guess where the pitcher's gonna pitch it, just hit it where the pitcher pitches it."

Another coach told his pitcher, "The batter won't hit it if you throw it where he can't."

Mayor Mongrel J. Clown came up to me, in full umpire regalia. "I thought you might like to know I'm a huge fan of yours," he said through his mask. "I liked that one funny sitcom you wrote."

"*The Nut Factory*?" I assumed.

"No, that's not it. It'll come to me."

"I'll wait."

The Mayor removed his mask, gave me a wink and leered, "You ever fuck a movie star?"

"Only if she insisted."

"I get off watching those Marilyn Monroe movies."

"I never masturbate to married women."

"Yeah, wouldn't be ethical," he absently acknowledged. "Y'know, my second cousin's brother-in-law's step-sister is in the show business."

"Is that so?"

"She did a toothpaste commercial."

"So you had a brush with fame," I noted.

Mayor Clown totally missed the joke and said, "You're taking on an impossible job, McKay. This team is hopeless. A bunch of goof-offs, duds, no-talent bums. The last general manager ran for his life and I wouldn't blame you for getting out while the getting is good."

My attention was drawn to Leo stumbling out of the dugout, ready to deliver his welcome address to the players. He forgot to stop batting practice and took a line drive to his potbelly, knocking him to the ground. The team gathered around. Heinie told him to rub some dirt on it. Leo rubbed. A miraculous recovery as he managed to stand up and say, "Uh, gentlemen and gentlemen, I am your owner and glad to own you."

Leo pointed over at me. "And here to tell you more is your new general manager, Springer McKay."

Leo scooted off. I hadn't expected to speak, so I improvised some surefire lines from old movies, leading off with—"They say we're down. They say we're out. They say we're through, we're going nowhere. Well, I say whoever *they* are don't know who *you* are. You are a *team*! You care about each other. Trust each other. Together you will win because you have the talent, the desire, and you are all destined to be *millionaires!*"

A burst of hoots and hollers leaned the scoreboard another foot to the right.

"And, now, guys," I continued, "I would like you all to meet…"

Heinie Pratt stepped in front of me, shouting, "Pratt's the name, baseballs my game!" He doffed his cap. A frog sprung off his shiny dome. He got his laughs.

"Now, in case you boys hadn't heard," Heinie continued, "the hardest thing to do in baseball is to pitch and to hit or nothing much ever happens, which is why baseball is a game of failure and most of you are gonna wash out because you suck and it's time to join the real world, so forget everything you learned, start over, play hard, get a shave and a haircut and have fun out there."

Heinie Pratt doesn't breathe when he talks. Doesn't stop for periods. He talks loud, then soft. Keeps gabbling on. Makes just enough sense to bewilder.

CHAPTER SIX

I was smacking balls to my outfielders with limited success when this leathery face appeared before me. Snowy hair, frosty moustache, a beer-laden gut plopped over his uniform pants. He was whittling the face of Abraham Lincoln on a hunk of wood. Abe was grinning.

"Name's Doody, Max Doody," he informed me with Bronx in his voice. "I'm the battin' coach, and what in hell you doin' here? You're not a baseball man. You got no right to run this team. I gave my life to this game. Sixteen years in the minors. Been a *Mud Hen*, a *Canary*, a *Saltdog*, and a *Wingnut*. The *Dodgers* called me up, I hit .105 and I wonder whatever happened to me?" He spewed a lunger of tobacco juice into a plastic cup.

I pointed to the wad in his cheek. "That stuff'll kill ya."

"Yeah, I know," he muttered. "Chaw ain't as good as it used to be."

"Planning to quit?"

"Soon as I break the habit."

He spewed a bonus lunger and said, "I hope you know what you signed up for. This here team is the kindergarten of baseball. Boys hopin' to make it to the minors, so they can make it to the majors. It's a long ladder to the top. Most guys quit. But don't go gettin' the wrong idea. This team is better than our record and one'a these days we're gonna prove it."

Doody called my attention to a wiry young man artfully scooping up ground balls. "See Cabrera out there, only sixteen, hitch-hiked to the U.S. on a raft. Quick feet, soft hands, knows the pitches he can handle. Major League if I ever saw one."

He turned to a boy taking powerful swings at home plate. "That young buck jackin' balls out'a here, that's Noodles Weaver. Big for his age. Big for any age. Gonna put up numbers that'll pop your eyes out."

"That boy scoopin' up a ground ball?" he went on. "That's Scraps Wisenheimer. Plays a first-rate second base. Sees the ball well at the plate when it doesn't hit him. Hot on the temper side."

Doody indicated a goofy squirt in the outfield. "That's Iggy Fanoki makin' that divin' catch in center. Got pig flop for brains, but his talent makes up for it."

"Now, movin' from the plus to the minus," Doody chattered on, "that kid striking out is our first baseman Beans Bonano. He's in a battin' slump. Thinks he lost his talent."

Doody went on. "That youngster droppin' the fly ball in right field, that's Irving Melman. Likable lad. Great spirit. Strikes out a lot. Says he's a rabbi in case baseball doesn't work out which might turn out to be a wise prediction."

Doody continued to enlighten me. "See that fella bootin' that ground ball over on third base? That's Duke Rudolf. One of the older boys. Good hitter. Says he's a lawyer, but can't defend the fact he's leadin' the league in errors."

Doody gestured to the stumpy young man crouched behind the plate. "That there is Stubby Jenks. Been here four seasons. A fine catcher, hitter, knows baseball, reliable as a rock."

Doody drilled me a dead-level look and said, "I should be the manager of this club, ya know. I played with Heinie Pratt. If he hadn't been a fan favorite they would have locked him in the looney bin."

He spewed a final lunger and lumbered off.

A grayish brillo-headed beanpole loped up to me. Six-ten, long stringy arms, a nose that could flip bottle caps. Through the toothy smile of a chipmunk, he said, "Hi, I'm Spook Spindler, your pitching coach. You probably remember me from my appearance in the World Series...Bottom of the ninth. Had a no-hit game in progress, one out to go, and a home run expunges my rightful place as a baseball legend...So what's *your* story? What is Mister Hollywood doing running this team? Are you out of your mind?"

"The jury's still out."

Spook pointed to the tall, good-looking Black kid warming up. "That big right-hander over there, that's Streamline West. Says he was born on a train going west at the time. A natural on the mound. Nineteen, grows a little everyday. A possible Cy Young if he stops talking to himself on the mound. Batters read lips."

Spook continued. "That older fellow next to West is Virgil Weathers. Lost his fastball, his curve, fighting to return to the majors, and that knuckleball I'm teaching him is going get him there…Next to Virgil, that youngster hurling rockets is Ron Rigler. Already clocked at ninety-seven. I tell him to ease up, he says he can't help it, he's naturally brilliant."

"The rest of my pitching staff comes and goes. But, someday, when that scout comes poking around, I want my boys to shine, and that won't happen with Heinie Pratt poisoning the well."

CHAPTER SEVEN

Mayor Mongrel J. Clown boomed into his megaphone, welcoming the sparse crowd to—"today's game between the *West Sweden Sturgeons* and our very own *Clowntown Clowns!*"

He announced the *Clowns'* starting lineup —

Allstate Cabrera at shortstop.

Scraps Wisenheimer at second.

Iggy Fanoki in center.

Noodles Weaver in left.

Stubby Jenks catching.

Duke Rudolf at third.

Beans Bonano at first.

Irving Melman in right.

On the mound, left-hander Streamline West.

The starting pitcher for the *Sturgeons* was right-hander Anger Thunstrom, better known as "Godzilla."

Mayor Clown went on to introduce The Clownzinger Family Singers who raised their voices in mangling *The Star-Spangled Banner*. The armed fans fired their weapons in the air to demonstrate their patriotism. A dead eagle landed on home plate.

In the first inning, Streamline West gave up a bases-loaded home run and things went downhill from there.

The team wasn't totally to blame, the Mayor made a load of bad calls against us, and when the *Sturgeons* scored their sixth run, Heinie Pratt turned pruney and charged out to reason with the Mayor.

"You loggerheaded plunderfart!" Heinie reasoned. "Can't tell a strike from a ball cuz you're a toad-brained clodpole who should get yourself a new set'a beady eyes!"

Mayor drew back. "How dare you talk to me like that! Do you know who I am?"

"You're a bubble ass!" Heinie blasted.

"Well, you're a *double* bubble ass!" the Mayor skillfully volleyed.

Heinie kicked dirt! The Mayor kicked dirt!

Heinie snatched up the garden hose, soaked the Mayor, who ejected him, which led to my boys committing blunders, gaffes, goofs…Final score—*Sturgeons* 14, *Clowns* 2, for which we received a standing *"BOO!"*

The clubhouse was soaked in shame. Heinie Pratt sat alone at his corner desk, slandering the Mayor with colorful phrases like…"Foot-lickin' pignut"…"Slobber-brained varlet"…"Lily-livered prickmonger…"

It ain't Shakespeare, but it's close.

First baseman Beans Bonano addressed the group. "I'm twenty-seven years old, I'd like a job with a future." He snatched up his gym bag and walked into *Clown* history.

The bright spots in today's game were a double, a triple and a home run by *Clowns* leftfielder Noodles Weaver, a Vikingish young man, with the bulging arms of Popeye.

I joined him at his locker. "Nice job out there, Noodles."

"Thanks," he bashfully replied. "My real name is Stanley. People call me Noodles 'cause I carbo-load."

To prove it he dug into a heaping plate of Kraft mac and cheese. "I know who you are," he said with a mouthful, "I grew up with your TV shows. *The Nut Factory* was my favorite. So, what are you doing here?"

"Searching for winning ways."

"The team sure could use some of those," he said. "We're trying the best we can. We all want to make it to the big leagues. It's been my dream since I was born, and it's gonna come true because I believe with all my heart that I have what it takes to make it to the majors."

"My boy's a cinch to do just that," piped a voice from a man pushing forty, who bore an undeniable resemblance to Noodles.

Warren Weaver introduced himself and said, "You take care of my boy, McKay. He's a gem. Gonna be a breakout star, isn't that right, son?"

"Sure thing, dad," said Noodles as he trotted off.

Warren lasered me a look and said, "I had a future in baseball before I got hurt. Ended up teaching science to fat-headed gnomes in Connersville, Indiana. That's not happening to Noodles. Don't fuck up his chances."

Since Beans Bonano quit, we've tried several local boys at first base, none of them could get the hang of it, until this sweet-faced kid, toting a beat-up suitcase, walked onto the field. He looked about twelve, says he's eighteen, has farm boy written all over him. His name is Cookie Calaboosa. He plays first base.

Not only can Cookie play first, he can hit. And, if this seems like a coincidence, that's exactly what it was.

CHAPTER EIGHT

Three in the morning, in the midst of a dream where I'm honeymooning with Uma Thurman, there was a frantic rapping at my door.

There stood Leo in Spiderman pjs, terror in his eyes. He held up a baseball and wailed—*"Somebody threw this through my window!"*

"It could have been a wild pitch," I offered.

Leo started to laugh, stopped, "Don't try to cheer me up." He handed me the ball. "Here, read this."

Scrawled on the ball were the words—*"Quit now or else!"*

Leo trembled. "What do you think that means?"

"It means quit now or else."

"Or else what?"

"Someone doesn't want us here."

"Who?"

"Look, it's probably a joke. Just stay calm."

Leo was not calm. "Oh, sure, stay calm! Stay calm! How can I stay calm when 'or else' is about to happen? I never should've got myself into this. What do I know about baseball? My team got a standing boo! A boo is not entertainment. The public wants to be entertained."

"How about a mascot?" I suggested.

"What kind of mascot?"

"Isn't it obvious?"

"Sure it is," he said…"So what is it?"

"A *clown!*"

"Of course!" Leo beamed. "I was born to be a clown!"

Today's game against the *Dead Lake Loons* was scoreless into the fourth inning. Play was interrupted when a man somersaulted out of the stands and scampered onto the field. The man wore Clown make-up. Not a happy Clown. Grim. Like Leo's logo.

The Clown waddled around in huge flappy shoes and an oversized baseball uniform with a question mark on the back. His cap was askew. He held an oversized glove and a bat taller than he was. He trotted to the mound, "*quacked*" on a duck call, did an exaggerated wind-up—pitched—followed an imaginary ball to the plate, held his bat at the wrong end, swung, dropped his pants, did a pratfall. The handful of fans in attendance exploded with laughter!

Perched on the edge of the dugout, Heinie Pratt was not amused.

As for me, I could not believe Leo could do the things he was doing, so imagine my surprise when he appeared next to me while the Clown scooted around the ballpark handing out business cards —

Nutty Nuckleball!

The Clown Prince of Baseball!

"Leo," I said, "that Clown, I thought it was you."

"Nope," he replied, "he showed up, did his act, I hired him on the spot. We got ourselves a mascot, partner. Let the circus begin!"

The circus began with Heinie storming out of the dugout, throwing Nutty Nuckleball to the ground, and pounding him with his fists while hollering—"*I hate clowns!*"

Heinie was ejected and left the field to chants of —"*We hate Heinie!*"

The team actually played better after Heinie was tossed. No errors. The *Dead Lake Loons* beat us by only three runs. There's reason for optimism.

Back in the clubhouse, Heinie took Leo and me aside to lay down the law. "That Clown is makin' mock, don't need his kind'a foolshit, I want him gone—vamoosed—defunct!!"

Heinie stormed off yanking his dark cloud with him.

Leo turned to me and pleaded. "I can't get rid of Nutty. I gave him a five-year contract. Do you know how embarrassing it would be to get sued by a Clown?"

"A pie in the face for sure."

Nutty Nuckleball was a sensation! His routines grew increasingly creative. Today, he ran out to second base—threw a baseball behind his back—a *strike* to home plate. He suddenly stepped up to the plate in the bottom of the ninth and belted one into the seats to win the game. Later reversed because the Nutty wasn't on the team.

Attendance shot up. Nutty noses, duck calls, red-wigged Nutty caps went on sale at unreasonable prices…all bearing the grim visage of a creepy Clown.

CHAPTER NINE

Heinie's repeated attempts to force Nutty off the field were backfiring with the fans. *"Dump Pratt"* signs were popping up everywhere.

The situation had Leo at looser ends than usual. He begged me to do something. I suggested we talk to Nutty, ask him to tone it down… But how can a Clown tone it down? If a Clown tones it down, there's no Clown to tone down.

Nevertheless, Leo and I held a private meeting with Nutty in the clubhouse. I tried drawing him into a conversation but he would not be drawn. He spoke in mime, made silly faces, duck calls, pratfalls. He concluded his act by somersaulting out the door.

Seconds later, Heinie Pratt stormed in and dumped bits of paper in front of us.

"What's this?" I asked.

"My contract," Heinie growled. "Fire the clown and I'll glue it together."

Leo's eyes bulged in panic. "No, Heinie! I…I can't fire Nutty."

"*Mister* Pratt to you, nutworm!" Heinie barked. "That Clown is screwin' with my team cuz just when my boys wanna be discovered by the biggies that goofball is pilferin' their thunder and if he don't get the hell out'a here there's no tellin' what I'm gonna do!"

"But Mister Pratt," Leo begged, "Nutty is a mute and we have to do our part to help the handicapped."

Heinie covered his ears and like a stubborn little boy, bawled out—*"I can't hear you!"*

It was unfortunate to schedule a game the day of the Annual Clowntown Shootdown.

Sell-out crowd. Top of seventh. Streamline West shutting out the *Beaverbrook Bullheads* 4-0.

Suddenly—a deer *crashed* through the outfield wall and ran haphazardly around the park, looking for a way out. Fans in the stands fired shots at the animal and missed.

Nutty Nuckleball somersaulted onto the field. He approached the deer waving his polka dot hanky like a bullfighter. The deer lunged at Nutty, Nutty waved. Another lunge, another wave. The fans loved it!

Nutty bowed to acknowledge the cheers. The deer dove forward, his antlers pinning Nutty against the stands.

Nutty snatched a shotgun from a fan.

The deer was a dead duck.

Nutty took another bow, suddenly grabbed his neck, staggered around like a drunk, and did a pratfall to waves of laughter!

…Several minutes passed. The Clown didn't move. Just sat there.

Nutty had pratted his final fall.

CHAPTER TEN

The game was suspended. Nutty was dead. I had to know why.

I paid a call on Sheriff Gus Clowndale, a skittery young dude, practicing a quick draw with his six-gun. A huge Stetson covered his ears.

The Sheriff knew who I was. Told me it is his sworn duty to know about everybody and everything in the community he serves. He prides himself on being the CSI of Clown County, and is equally proud to be the town historian with a wealth of knowledge he likes to share with strangers.

"Like, for instance," he began in his whipsnappy voice, "in the early days of Clowntown everybody's last name was Clown in honor of our founder, Mongrel J. Clown. Then, when it was learned that Mongrel J. Clown had a screw loose what with torturing Indians, burning witches and all, a lot of the citizens changed their names. We got Clownmans, Clownwicks, Clownfinkels, Clowndinkels, you name it."

I thanked Sheriff Clowndale for that peculiar bit of intelligence, told him I was there about Nutty Nuckleball's unfortunate demise.

"Well, according to my calculations," he said. "it was a hunting accident. Happens all the time. Folks don't know how to aim. You shoot a bullet in the air, it's got to land somewheres, so I thought maybe this Nutty guy might have expired from a falling bullet, but I can't find a bullet wound. Here, let me show you."

The Sheriff led me to an adjoining room, lifted the lid of a super-sized freezer where Nutty laid next to a gallon of rocky road. The clown make-up had been removed revealing the freezer-burned face of a dead guy who could easily pass for no one in particular.

"All he had on him was twelve dollars and an AARP card," the Sheriff told me. "The card says his name is Tinky Farzock. Could be a hobo from the other side of where the tracks used to be."

A defrosted Nutty Nuckleball, aka Tinky Farzock, was to lie in state in full clown make-up and, due to my vast show business experience, Leo volunteered me to do the job.

So there I was at the Clowntown Morgue, smearing white on Nutty's face, when something on his neck caught my eye. Looked like a zit. Upon closer observation it appeared to be a puncture wound. A puncture wound...? This might require further examination.

Nutty's funeral was held at the Clowngrave Funeral Home on Gopher Walloon Drive. Mayor Clown was selling tickets at the door. An army of gun-toting fans packed the pews.

The reverend Somber J. Clownright, an Uzi strapped to his back, droned a solemn eulogy, ending with..."God himself brought Nutty Nuckleball to our fair community. And, in this silly man's brief moment amongst us, we experienced joy, we got the joke, and will laugh forever after, amen...And now the Clownzinger Family Singers, assisted by the Clowntown Drum and Tuba Corps, will present their rendition of *Be a Clown, be a Clown, all the world loves a Clown.*"

You had to be there.

A reception followed in the basement featuring a life-sized facsimile of Nutty Nuckleball in raw hamburger. Crackers were provided as a line of mourners helped themselves to cannibal sandwiches.

I snuck upstairs to collect some badly needed evidence. Found Nutty's open casket in the post-slumber room. Using my Swiss Army knife, I peeled away a sample of the puncture wound, placed the sample in a

Ziploc snack bag, closed the casket, and fled to the bathroom to recycle my cannibal sandwich.

The Google Girl directed Wolfgang to the itty-bitty Clowntown Post Office where I expressed Nutty's skin sample to Ralph Dalton Futz, a colleague who writes murder mysteries and thinks he's Sherlock Holmes. Futz was actually committed at one point, but he figured a way out, and if anyone can un-riddle a riddle it's riddler Ralph.

I called Futz, filled him in on the murder, I needed his help.

Intrigued by the idea, he said, "Elementary, my dear Springer, let us hatch ourselves a plot!"

CHAPTER ELEVEN

The injuries are piling up. Several boys are on the disabled list.

Heinie thundered up to me and said, "I'm down to nine ballplayers, anybody breaks an arm or a head I got no team, can't win with no team, need players, get me players."

I promised I'd get him players. Where do I get players?

I took out a "Ballplayers Wanted" ad in the *Clowntown Daily Tattler*. Two locals showed up. The first was a large, hawk-nosed man firmly in his eighties. Said his name was Bob Snooks. Square-shouldered with a mane of white hair, he claimed he was ready to play. Even had a note from his doctor telling me it was okay to put him in the line-up. To prove it he did thirty push-ups, forty sit-ups and, when he twirled me over his head to show me his wrestling skills, I gave him a shot.

Snooks hit my first pitch clear into the woods behind the outfield wall. Same with the second. The third. I told him I would definitely keep him in mind."

"No, you won't," he said.

"Why not?"

"I'm the town drunk."

The second applicant was a huskily winsome young woman of seventeen who told me she was the left-handed pitching ace the *Clowns* are desperately in need of.

It would've been bad-mannered to blow her off, so I grabbed a catcher's mitt and challenged her to prove it.

Her fastball knocked me over.

Her change-up would still be floating in if I hadn't leapt forward to snag it.

She snapped me a slider that dropped like a rock, bouncing off the plate to where I forgot to wear a cup.

I writhed on the ground…Ohhhmigod…….

The girl ran up, flushed with achievement. "Pretty nifty, huh?"

"Uh-huh," I chirped like a soprano. "How did you learn to pitch like that?"

"It comes naturally," she said. "I am what is known as a fee-nom."

"Yeah, right," I agreed as my balls showed signs of life. "Who are you?"

"Billie Bedwedder," she said. "I'm a senior at Clowntown High and I'm gonna show the boys I'm better than they are."

"Good plan if the boys'll let you."

"That's where you come in," she said. "You're a boy. You can ignite a baseball revolution. Hurl a high hard one through that glass ceiling. I don't throw like a girl, even though it's a more natural motion for the human arm. And I don't throw like a boy and hurt myself and have operations. I'm young, durable, a born fireballer, so next time wear a cup."

"Billie," I had to level, "I'm not sure there will be a next time."

"Sure there will," she said with certainty. "In the nineteen-fifties, Toni Stone and Connie Morgan of the *Indianapolis Clowns* played alongside the boys, so with history on my side, it's time for my chance."

"Look, you're only seventeen…"

"I could pass for eighteen."

"Billie, you're a very impressive talent, and I promise I'll think it over."

"No you won't. You're a bigot."

"I'm not a bigot."

She ran off, shouting—"You're nothing but an ignorant tool of absurdity!"

I was left to wonder if she was right.

CHAPTER TWELVE

I'm soapy in the shower. My phone rings. I soaked the carpet. "Yeah?" I answered with drippy irritation.

My mother. Wants me to call her back. I call her back. She's worried about me. "I'm fine," I told her.

"No, you're not," she insisted. "This baseball thing. It's cuckoo-bonkers. What does my son know about baseball?"

"I played baseball, mom."

"You were a total disgrace."

"I almost hit a home run."

"Then you struck out."

"Stop worrying, mom, I can handle it."

"Comedy you can handle," she stated. "Baseball I'm not so sure."

I don't know what it is, but ever since mom moved to Florida she's become my Jewish mother.

I returned to my shower. Phone rings. Soaked the carpet. "Whaddya want!" I snapped.

It was my colleague, Ralph Dalton Futz with information on the Nuckleball case. "The skin sample you sent me has a residue of rare poison called curare'," he crisply informed me. "Are you familiar with it?"

"Sure am," I stated. "It was the fatal poison in *The Feathered Serpent* with Roland Winters as Charlie Chan and Mantan Moreland as his hilarious sidekick, Birmingham."

"The Chan films were always an entertaining blend of comedy and murder," Futz acknowledged, going on to say—"Curare', better known as strychnos toxifera, is an extremely potent plant extract from the jungles of the Amazon from which isoquinoline and indole alkaloids are isolated."

"This poison," he continued, "causes the victim to undergo weakness of the skeletal muscles, resulting in paralysis of the diaphragm, leading to asphyxiation and certain death. Small doses of curare' have also been used in hospitals as a muscle relaxant, although I much prefer a morphine drip."

I thanked Futz for the info.

It will be added to my bill for his services.

Our suspended game resumed in top of the seventh inning with Streamline West shutting out the *Beaverbrook Bullheads* 4-0.

...Not for long. A jumble of walks, hits and errors had the *Bullheads* scuttling the *Clowns* 5-4.

Back in the clubhouse, a naked Heinie Pratt, his considerable penis swinging like a pendulum, delivered his postgame analysis to the players. "You're playin' like humpty dumptys, a bunch'a paddywacks who shouldn't have numbers you should have fractions cuz you don't stay new for long in baseball and I ain't lettin' my mind wander to where did you leave your heads, not in the game that's for sure, and if I had a good mind I'd trade you all to the fuckup league!"

Having successfully sucked the air out of the room Heinie walked away, displaying a tattoo of a snake entering his ass from the left and exiting his ass on the right.

But enough about that, I had to cut through this mopey fog. My boys need encouragement and I have experience in this area. After mom divorced dad she relied on me to help bring up my brothers. Now it's up to me to bring up these boys.

Streamline West stood silently staring at his locker. The kid is at least six-nine. Ties his shoes without bending. Whoever created this specimen over-extended themselves.

"You'll get 'em next time," I said.

Streamline didn't respond.

"Just turn the page," I told him.

Still no response.

"It's the next game that counts," I added.

Streamline remained silent.

"*Say something*," I pleaded. "I'm running out of clichés."

"My fastball wasn't," he muttered. "My curveball didn't. That wild pitch killed me."

"Had a lot on it," I said. "Sailed to the back row."

Streamline jerked a look at me, his chiseled features clenched in a scowl. "Why are you talking to me? The last GM never talked to me."

"He didn't have my big mouth," I said.

"Well, what's there to talk about?" he scoffed. "I'll never learn how to pitch. I should've taken that chemistry scholarship. Could've won a Nobel Prize."

"Yeah," I nodded, "that's always an option."

"I don't *want* an option!" Streamline insisted. "I am going to pitch in the major leagues!"

"That's the spirit," I cheered. "The next time you get up on that mound I want you to stare down that batter with a look that says—*Home plate is mine and you can't take it away.*"

Streamline looked doubtful. "Why would that work?"

"Because a pitcher knows and a batter guesses."

Enter our pugged-nosed catcher, Stubby Jenks. Stocky, shaved head, he chattered to Streamline in a raspy voice—"Ya know, sometimes life is like a reality show no matter how much it sucks. But I'm a positive sort of guy. I try to be positive where ever I go. Whenever I see somebody that's down I go up to that person and give them my positive energy, and that's what I'm doin' right now, so let's you and me have a little chat."

Stubby threw a friendly arm around Streamline. They walked off in animated conversation.

Clowns' slugger Noodles Weaver walked up to me and said, "Sorry about losing, Mister McKay."

Warren appeared at his side. "Never be sorry, son," he advised, "you did your part today." He turned to me, "How about my boy's performance? All four runs belong to him."

"It's for the team, dad," Noodles nobly stated. "I did it for the team."

"And soon it'll be a Major League team," Warren declared. "We're going for that billion dollar prize, son. Nothing can stop us. Great days ahead."

CHAPTER THIRTEEN

My ears were rattled by a loud *banging*! The source of the banging was our second baseman, Scraps Wisenheimer, butting his flaming red head against his locker.

Figuring I should speak up, I did. "Sorry to bother you, Scraps, but you may need your head for tomorrow's game."

He kept butting, so I told him, "Keep it up and you'll knock your freckles off."

Scraps stopped and pouted—"Oh for five! I get a shave and a haircut and just like Samson in that old movie I got no strength, no talent, all I got is a headache!"

Iggy Fanoki, this bug-eyed youngster with pointy hair and a constant look of surprise, walked up to me, lowered his head and stammered…"You think I'm toe jam, dont'cha?"

"Why would I think that?"

"Cause I am," he gloomed. "Three errors today. I'm scared stiff. All those crazies in the stands with guns. One more goof and I'm a head on a wall."

I was not excepting our Dominican shortstop, Allstate Cabrera, to slide headfirst through my legs, but that's what he did. A good-looking kid with bleached blonde hair, he sprung up, gave me a welcoming hug and a grin reminiscent of licorice Chicklets.

Our tall, nattily attired, third baseman Duke Rudolf came over and, in his deeply resonant voice, explained, "Allstate speaks Spanish and I'm teaching him English."

"Fuck you mother," Allstate grinned.

"We still have a ways to go," Duke explained.

"How did he get a name like Allstate?" I wondered.

"His real name is Juan," said Duke, "but he wants to sound American and nothing says American like Allstate."

Our nine-year-old batboy, Peewee, was busy collecting towels off the dirt floor. Peewee's a nickname the players hung on him. His real name is Merton, he prefers Peewee. Blonde, crew cut, tops the chart at four feet, even though he claims to be four-feet-one-and-a-half, and four-feet-two-and-a-half when he wakes up in the morning because you get taller when you sleep and shrink when you stand up.

Peewee is proud to be our equipment manager, janitor, and target of pranks. Yesterday, Virgil Weathers sent Peewee to get a box of curveballs. Day before that, Iggy Fanoki told him to find him the key to the batter's box. Peewee knew he'd been pranked, but he laughed harder than anybody. He worships his buddies, his heroes, these honest-to-goodness ballplayers who will someday be famous, and maybe so will he.

Before today's game, I found Peewee on the bench, jamming a chaw of tobacco in his mouth. This seriously concerned me. I don't like to see boys, even girls, chewing tobacco, so I broached the subject.

"Peewee," I began, "about the tobacco..."

He interrupted. "I know what you're gonna say, Mister McKay, my mom and dad don't like it either."

"Good," I nodded, "then you'll give it up."

"Not yet," said Peewee. "Coach Doody told me never to quit until I can do it without throwing up on his shoes, so that's my goal."

Peewee jammed more chaw in his cheek, chawed, and chawed, and threw up on my shoes.

CHAPTER FOURTEEN

Heinie Pratt had installed his office in a dark corner of the clubhouse. He communicated with the players by yelling things like—"The asshole who left his turd on my desk better come and get it." Snickers from the boys.

Meantime, I sat alone at my locker, wracking my brain for ways to improve my team's chances. To see these boys get their dream was now a dream of mine. Should I chance another ad in the paper hoping the ghost of Mickey Mantle shows up? Or have a mystic bring back Dizzy Dean?... I couldn't concentrate. My mind was on my case. I didn't expect to have a case, but murder seems to show up wherever I go.

I paid a call on Sheriff Clowndale to fill him in. "What I know so far is Nutty Nuckleball died from a puncture wound to the neck. The puncture shows evidence of curare' poisoning."

The Sheriff's eyes brightened. "You think maybe it was caused by some exotic murder weapon?"

"I'm not sure. It could be as simple as a pea from a shooter."

We lost to the *Timberville Splinters* by a score of 9 to 3. Our team scored on a three-run jack from Noodles Weaver. The *Splinters* scored with hit batters, wild pitches, and home runs served up by our veteran starter, Virgil Weathers.

In the clubhouse, after the game, a fist fight broke out between Virgil and Ron Rigler.

Heinie Pratt made no move to stop the action, ordering everyone to—"Let the dicks duke it out!"

I figured I could either step in and lose my newly-expensive bridge or do something else. I chose something else and burst into song.

"*Swaaaaneeee! How I love ya, how I love ya, my dear old Swanee! I'd give the world to beeeee among the folks in D-I-X-* ..." and before I got to *"I-E"* the guys stopped fighting and gawked at me proving that tone-deafness has its advantages.

The fight morphed into a verbal sparring match.

"Give it up, old man!" Rigler shouted at Virgil.

"I ain't no quitter!" Virgil shouted back.

"Could've fooled me," taunted Rigler.

"I pitched in the Majors," Virgil stated, "how about you?"

"Ancient history, has-been," Rigler snapped. "Whenever you pitch we're always behind and I'm a closer with nothing to close. I am destined to be a star, and I am not going to let a loser like you get in my way."

The sparring match became a staring match.

Rigler was the first to blink. "Fuck off, asswipe!"

Virgil deftly countered with, "Same to you, bully boy!"

Asswipe and bully boy retired to their lockers.

Leo Merkin skittered up in panic mode. "Springer, I don't like the looks of this. We gotta do something."

"Good idea," I agreed. "Let's go talk to them."

Leo drew back. "Oh, no, I don't do well in confrontations. I got kicked off the debate team because I lost on purpose."

"Leo, it's time you got to know your players."

"I'm an owner," he explained. "I don't have to know my players, I just have to be rich."

Leo fled to wherever Leo flees to.

Virgil Weathers was seated at his locker. Slender, balding, wire-rimmed glasses nested on his narrow nose. He had an icepack strapped to his right arm and was struggling to get dressed.

Helping him into his shirt, I spotted his younger image on the baseball card taped to his locker. "I saw you pitch in the Majors."

He turned to me with a broad smile, and drawled, "Ya'll saw me?"

"At Dodger Stadium. You shut-out the Giants."

"Yeah, I had everything goin' that day," he beamed. "My sinker sunk, fastball was a pill, change-up crossed the plate the next day…Then my arm got sore. Got sent down to work it out. Still tryin' to work it out. But I ain't complain'. No reason to worry none. I'll just keep goin', keep workin'. Got a wife and five kids. Need that paycheck."

CHAPTER FIFTEEN

I took a long look at Ron Rigler—he was very long to look at. At only nineteen, he stood at six-four, two-thirty. Devilishly handsome in tinted aviator glasses. He sauntered over, slapped my back, I swallowed my gum.

"I know, what you're thinking, McKay," he said, "people always take me for a movie star."

"It's a cross you'll have to bear."

"As you have no doubt seen by now." Rigler continued, "I throw smoke. Explode the radar gun. A *New York Yankee* scout tried to sign me at sixteen, but I was smart. I knew I wasn't ready, wasn't mature, but now I am ready, I am electric, I am the next best thing!"

Rigler rolled up the sleeve of his jersey, placed my hand on his arm and said, "Feel the power. Armed and dangerous!"

"Don't be shy young man. I'll bet you have a plan."

"Of course I do," Rigler confirmed. "After my brief stay in this rock bottom hellhole, a major league scout will honor me with an enormous signing bonus, followed by one month of seasoning in Triple A where I will rocket to major league millions, enjoy a twenty-year career, a huge pension, star on my own TV show, I'm a fast-tracking dude!"

"And when they make the movie of your life, you can play yourself."

"That's part of my plan," he snappily replied, "and you can help. Get this team some offense. Guys who can hit. Guys who can give me a lead to protect. My future's in your hands, McKay, don't let me down."

Our right fielder, Irving Melman, was killing off a bag of Wavy Lays. Twenty, maybe more. Doesn't look like a ballplayer, more like a baker who eats all the profits.

He wore ear buds, off in his own world. He twinkled me a smile, removed the buds and said, "Listening to *Gypsy*. One of the finest scores in the American musical theatre with the possible exception of *Fiddler on the Roof*, *My Fair Lady*, *The Music Man*, *West Side Story*, *Guys & Dolls*, *The Most Happy Fella*, I could go on all day."

"I'll bet you could, Irving," I said. "Or should call you Rabbi?"

"Ah, yes," he grinned, "the boys like to kid me about being a rabbi."

"You really *are* a rabbi?"

"Indeed I am," he affirmed. "I did my online studies with the Schmeeler Rabbinical School in Tel Aviv. If baseball doesn't work out I can always fall back on faith."

We beat the *Scum River Cavaliers* by a score of 7 to 2. The winning pitcher was Streamline West. Ron Rigler registered a save.

The clubhouse rocked! Doctor Pepper was sprayed in my face, followed by a stinging barrage of peas! I glanced around to spot the shooter only to find that everyone in the room, including Heinie Pratt, had a pea shooter in his hand.

I squished across the soda-soaked floor to Cookie Calaboosa and asked, "What's with the pea shooters?"

"Well, baseball's a kid's game." Cookie explained, "and all us kids got toys."

Scraps Wisenheimer nudged me. "And some of the toys are *girls*…if ya know what I mean."

"You think it's right to call a girl a toy?" I asked.

"They're toys if you meet 'em at the Animal Bar," Scraps winked. "You should come out, treat yourself to a good time…if ya know what I mean."

CHAPTER SIXTEEN

Deep in the woods, a flashing neon sign proclaimed —

NUDE GIRLS NIGHTLY!!

Which led me to suspect the Animal Bar was a strip joint.

The "*boom-thumpa-boom*" music added to that suspicion.

Photos of scantily-clad young women were displayed at the entrance with names like *Cricket, Luscious, Exotica, Chastity, Destiny, the Schnitzel Sisters* (*Brunhilda & Brunhelga*), and *Cloris, the bow-legged contortionist*.

At the entrance stood Max Doody in his *Clown* cap, Hawaiian shirt, a forty-five strapped to his side. "What're you doin' here, McKay?" he asked.

"Isn't this the library?" I replied.

"Lemme see your ID."

"What for?"

"I'm the bouncer."

"Moonlighting?"

"Can't make no livin' coachin' *Clowns*."

I handed Doody my California license. He stared holes through it and remarked, "You look younger for your age."

"And I plan to keep it that way."

Once my eyes adjusted to the purplish lighting I could clearly see the walls were clogged with heads. Deer, bears, badgers, beavers, moose and a squirrel glared at me in taxidermic shock.

Other heads were attached to the Schnitzel Sisters who danced around me twirling their tassels with verve and vivation!

The Animal Bar offered a variety of activities.

Destiny, covered in balloons, handed out pins for pricking.

Chastity did push-ups on Duke's lap.

Allstate and Cloris, the bowlegged contortionist simulated sex on the dance floor.

Luscious led Heinie into a back room marked *Paradise*.

Stubby sat alone, engrossed in a comic book.

Noodles struggled to get the claw to pick up the stuffed monkey.

A number of men immersed themselves in roulette, slots, poker.

Iggy was losing at craps.

Soon as I grabbed a stool at the circular bar, a topless young woman threw her arms around me and bubbled—"Hi! I'm Destiny, your sales associate!"

My sales associate had cotton candy hair, make-up applied with a trowel, her g-string shrunk in the wash. "Buy me a drink?" she asked.

"Uh, yeah, sure."

"Dom Perignon over here!" she yelled.

The bartender appeared and, in a voice low and intense, she told Destiny to—"Leave this guy alone. He looks like he has class."

Destiny shot off to her next target.

"She's not your type," said the bartender, adding, "The name's Tempest and you're the new Clown-in-chief."

"How'd you know that?" I asked.

"Nothing escapes me," she said with the slyest of smiles.

This woman made a socko first impression. Cascading red hair, puckery mouth, sizable nose, one eye green, one blue, a stew of parts that collaborate exceptionally well.

"I never met a Tempest before."

"You now have that pleasure," she said. "You here with your wife?"

"Divorced."

"Me, too. He thought I was a rug he could walk all over."

"Married men make such poor husbands."

Her laugh was sincere, committed, I was smitten.

"*Tempest—stop yer flirtin'!*" screeched a voice. "*We need beer here!*"

"*Cork it, guzzlebutt!*" she snapped back.

She touched my arm, said, "Don't be a stranger," and got back to her job.

Behind me Scraps was intensely debating some local yokel, who growled, "We're tired'a you assholes comin' in here, and foolin' with our women."

To which Scraps sneered, "Well, maybe they're lookin' for some *real* men!"

The yokel replied with a right! Then a left! And a right! Another right! A left...! My second baseman was about to be chopped liver, so I stepped forward to make peace.

Another yokel blocked my way. "Stand back!" he ordered. "Let the *Clown* lose like the *Clowns* always lose."

I told the yokel to show some respect for my team. He replied with a swift uppercut to my jaw. Not one to fall unconscious I pushed the yokel into other yokels igniting a brawl with me and my boys as the feature attraction.

A *GUNSHOT* shook the rafters! The fighting stopped. Tempest stood atop the bar brandishing a huge revolver.

"The next man to throw a punch will be disqualified from the meat raffle!" she shouted. "And no more picking on our *Clowntown Clowns*. The team may be shit and an embarrassment to our community, but there's a new man in charge and we're gonna have a winner or else. So smile, relax, get back to your fun and games."

The yokels did as they were told.

I rounded up my players. We carried Scraps' unconscious body out of the bar, piled him in Wolfgang's back seat.

Iggy, Stubby, Allstate, Duke and Noodles gathered around me, all smiles.

"Thanks for stickin' up for us, boss," said Stubby.

"We do appreciate it," added Duke.

"We feel like you're one of us now," grinned Noodles.

"I'm always looking out for my boys," I assured them.

"In that case," Iggy beamed, "could you give us a raise?"

CHAPTER SEVENTEEN

Got to my room around midnight. Found Leo Merkin facedown on my pillow. I lifted his head—"How did you get in? The door was locked."

He bolted upright, and flustered—"Your window is open. I'll pay for the damage."

"What are you doing here?"

"Nothing," he said, bursting into tears.

"Call me psychic, Leo, but I have a hunch something's wrong."

"Wrong?" he sniffled. "What could be wrong? Attendance sucks, that's what's wrong! We had fifteen fans at yesterday's game and I gave away fifty tickets. We need something to get people into the stands…so I wanna float this idea, see what you think."

"Lay it on, Leo," I said.

"We'll give away bobbleheads."

Leo handed me a bobblehead. I studied it. "This looks like you."

"Kind of."

"You look Chinese."

"All bobbleheads do."

"We can do better."

"But I bought ten-thousand."

"Put 'em on the back burner."

"They'll melt."

"Bobbleheads won't keep us from jumping off a cliff, Leo. You and only you can bring the fans back to the park."

"Nobody's gonna pay to see me play."

"You don't have to play, Leo. All you have to do is give your team a unifying spirit. They feel unappreciated by you."

"I know," Leo mumbled. "I'm rich. They hate me. It's lonely at one-percent."

"But you can earn their appreciation by opening your heart and raising their pay. If you give them a sense of worth, they'll have the will to win... And, while you're at it, we need a toilet seat, fresh towels, a shower that showers and wooden bats, aluminum lacks excitement."

Leo snickered to a chuckle. "Springer, my man," he said, "not a problem. I am a responsible owner. My players will get their raise."

"And a twelve bars of Lifebuoy." I added.

There was a rapping at my door, followed by the snappy voice of Sheriff Gus Clowndale. "You sleeping, McKay? Got something to show you!"

Leo began to twitch. "I gotta hide," he said. "Whenever I see a law enforcement officer I know I did something wrong."

He scooted under the bed. I answered the door.

"Sorry to bother you at this late hour," said Sheriff Clowndale, "but crime never sleeps."

He placed a detailed drawing of Clowntown Memorial Stadium on the bed. "I happen to be an amateur surveyor," he told me, "and according to my calculations Nutty Nuckleball, aka Tinky Farzock, was standing in point blank range of the *Clowns'* dugout when he was dispatched by a dart. The entry angle of said dart clearly shows it is more than likely a *Clowntown Clown* killed the clown."

"Impressive work, Sheriff...You think the murder weapon is a dart?"

"My best guesstimate is a poisoned dart from a blowgun, like in that old Charlie Chan movie. It makes sense and adds an element of intrigue to our case and, since it's gonna be a pretty intriguing case, I thought we should start by contacting the media, hold a press conference, maybe a shot on *60 Minutes*. It's not every day curare' kills a clown."

"True," I said, "but if we're going to face the media we've got to be prepared. There's a lot more to learn before we tell it all on *60 Minutes*. For now let's keep this under wraps."

Sheriff Clowndale seemed disappointed, but agreed, and left the room, muttering, "I've always wanted to be on *60 Minutes*..."

Leo's head popped out from under the bed—"Murder? Poison dart? Is there something I don't know?"

"You know now," I said, "and I want you to keep your trap shut. Not a word to anyone. Promise?"

"My lips are sealed."

"With glue if you blab."

I figured I'd send the drawing of Clown Memorial Stadium to Ralph Dalton Futz for confirmation. All I had to do was scan the document to a printer and, as luck would have it, Clownhowser's Bed & Barn had a Corporate Center. A pint-sized room off the lobby which consisted of a computer, a printer, and a framed photo of Senator Joe McCarthy.

I e-mailed the drawing along with a message asking Futz for any information he could find on a guy named Tinky Farzock.

Futz phoned me in no time at all, exclaiming—"Gadzooks! This drawing of Clown Memorial Stadium conclusively proves the guilty party or parties were indeed situated in the *Clown* dugout during the commission of this dastardly deed."

"As per your request," Futz blazed on, "here is what I have ascertained... As a boy Tinky Farzock was part of his family's circus act *The Flying Farzocks*. When he was sixteen he turned in his trapeze to pursue his love for baseball, spent several years in the minor leagues, and a few months at third base for the *Cincinnati Redlegs*, as they were known at that time. Tinky batted a paltry .085. *Cincinnati* sent him back to the minors where he gave up his quest for baseball immortality and attended The Skelton Clown Institute in Vincennes, Indiana, graduating with honors in duck calling...I am not joking, just stating facts."

"Upon graduation," Futz continued, "Tinky Farzock became Nutty Nuckleball, the Clown Prince of Baseball, touring small ballparks with his act, having had the misfortune to choose yours...I, therefore, urge you to forge onward with your inquiry, the answer is well within your grasp. My billable hours have been added to your account."

CHAPTER EIGHTEEN

Old Bob Snooks was at the entrance to the clubhouse swinging his hefty bat like a toothpick. "I'm on the wagon, McKay," he announced. "Sign me up!"

"Wish I could, Bob."

"I ain't old, I'm just a youngster with experience."

"Sorry, Bob."

"Age discrimination," he scolded. "That's what this is."

Snooks took a baseball out of his pocket, tossed it in the air and knocked it out of sight.

"Air mailed to China," he said as he trotted off.

A finger jabbed my back. It belonged to young Billie Bedwedder. "What do you think, Mister McKay?" she asked in a deep phoney voice.

She wanted to know what I thought of the fake beard and mustache she was wearing. She looked like a Hobbit. "Well, if it isn't Bilbo Baggins."

"I am no laughing matter, Mister McKay," Billie asserted, "I'm good enough to play with the boys. I'm a great pitcher. I am the *future!*"

"Yes, you are," I agreed. "I'll see you then."

"Honestly, you are soooooo obsolete," she pouted as she slumped off.

I entered the *Clown* clubhouse and was pleased to see a new toilet seat, working shower, fresh towels, four wooden bats and twelve bars of Lifebuoy.

Duke Rudolf was addressing his fellow players. "We make less than a fast food worker," he said. "Less than a cashier at Walmart. Something should be done about that, don't you agree?"

The guys nodded their agreement.

Ron Rigler strongly objected, calling Duke a "tree-hugging socialist."

Iggy Fanoki tugged at my sleeve, and said, "Mister McKay, I can't play today, I'm sick."

"What's wrong?" I asked with concern.

"I got gy-ne-phobia," he said.

"You have a fear of women?"

"Not a chance."

"Then you're not sick."

Iggy drifted off, murmuring to himself, "I got the wrong phobia..."

Scraps Wisenheimer stood before the cracked full-length mirror, poised to hit, his body shifting and twisting in reaction to imaginary fastballs.

"I'm practicin' gettin' hit by a pitch," Scraps explained to me. "It'll up my on-base percentage. The best place to get hit is from the shoulder blades to above the waist. Knees, elbows and knuckles are the worst. The ass is best unless you wanna sit down."

Scraps resumed his shifting and twisting.

Cookie Calaboosa sat at his locker, lips moving as he read from his ever-present Bible. He looked up at me and asked, "Mister McKay, do you think we encounter dead people when we go to heaven? Like, will my grandma be there to meet me at the gate?"

"Sure she will, unless she's late," I said. "I mean, with all the dead in heaven think of the gridlock. Like February in Florida."

Cookie thought that sort of made sense and went back to his Bible.

Coach Spook Spindler strode up to me, his hangdog face wrenched in a grin. "Good day, Springer McKay, I am your Rightway distributor with products guaranteed to give a lift to your life!"

He whipped open a shopping bag and began his pitch—"I've got Rock Solid energy bars that give you the strength of ten men. Gleemer toothpaste guaranteed to whiten and brighten your teeth. Blink laundry detergent. Your clothes won't stink when you use Blink. And how about DynaHealth vitamins, guaranteed to make you the sexual Superman you used to be. Not to mention, of course, a small volume by the founder of

Rightway, F. Ronnie Goniff." He held up a book entitled, *How I Did It and So Can You!*

"Can do what?" I asked.

"Can be your own boss," Spook professed. "Be an independent business owner. I'm an IBO, you're my recruit, I'll be your sponsor, get a percentage of the products you sell, and *you* get a percentage of the products *your* recruit sells, and what *his* recruit sells, and what *his* recruit sells, and so on and so forth, and we all get rewarded for helping the company grow. It's called relationship marketing."

"It's also called exploitation."

"What do you mean?"

"It's a Ponzi scheme."

"Like on *Happy Days*?"

"Not Fonzie—Ponzi. It's pyramid marketing."

"This has nothin' to do with Egypt."

"In that case, I'll pass."

Spook crammed his products in the bag, muttering, "Man-oh-man, try to boost our economy and this is the thanks I get."

Heinie Pratt was asleep at his corner desk, sputtering like a clogged drainpipe. I nudged him. "Heinie, you got a minute?"

Heinie slowly opened one eye, then another, and asked, "How are your bowels?"

"...As good as bowels go I guess."

"I haven't tooted a turd since I got here," Heinie complained, "feel like a stuffed turkey, I'll fart and blow the place up, so you're comin' to me because you want somethin' I can see it by your eyes, they used to call me eagle eye and I caught you eagle eyein' that bartender, sexy dangerous, I'd give her a tumble myself if I wasn't engaged to one of the young ladies."

"You're *what*? Engaged? To who?"

"Goes by the name of Luscious O'Boy," Heinie proudly announced. "She's my stress counselor and worships my magnificent body and you better believe there's nothin' wrong with contributin' to her college fund, she wants to be a jammer in the Roller Derby, so you want somethin' from me I can tell I have eagle eyes, I'm all ears."

He paused, all eyes and ears, so I said, "Heinie...do you think it's a good idea for the team to hang out at the Animal Bar? You're their manager. If you keep going there they'll follow your lead."

"Bet yer niblets they will," Heinie replied, "it was my idea for the boys to go there, get laid if they can afford it or settle for a complimentary blowjob cuz me and my boys are bonding, I'm gettin' their respect and you wouldn't want me to lose respect I'm a role model, so there's somethin' else you want I can tell I have eagle eyes."

"Okay, Heinie, there is something I want to ask you. Did you ever know a man by the name of Tinky Farzock?"

"If I knew some clown named Tinky I'd certainly know."

"So you knew Tinky was a clown?"

"Who the hell cares!" he roared. *"Everybody's* a clown in my book."

CHAPTER NINETEEN

Today we go up against our arch-rivals the *Kickapoo Hayhaulers* who the *Clowns* haven't beaten since Nixon left the White House.

Heinie gathered the players together for a talk. "Now, baseball is all about contriving and conniving and secret signs, I pull my ear means bunt, touch my nose don't bunt, rub my arm swing, tip my cap don't swing, except when I do the same sign, and the sign after that till there's no sign at all, so there's no thinkin' at the plate, you think at the plate, I'll never toot a turd."

The usual befuddled silence…Broken by Rabbi Melman who put down his Hostess Twinkie, stood up and rallied his teammates by singing— *"Things look swell, things look great, gonna have a big day at he plate, starting here, starting now, everything's coming up roses…!"*

He was pelted by baseball mitts.

Roses did not come up for the *Clowns* as we were spanked by the *Kickapoos* 6-2. Our team led 2-0 in the ninth inning and spirits were high until Ron Rigler came in to close and the *Hayhaulers* scored six unearned runs due to flukes, gaffes, boo-boos, not a joyful sight.

After the game Heinie Pratt gathered the team for another talk. "Now I ain't gonna go bawlin' you out when you should'a had the runs you gifted the opposition, I ain't gonna do that even though I should, so I want you to put it behind you, it never happened, it'll never happen again, and we should count our lucky stars to be in this land of loose women, always use a rubber, better safe than children, gotta go, gotta date." And off he went.

A dejected silence...No one said a word until Ron Rigler shouted—"You're all a bunch of losers! Duds! Deadbeats!"

Noodles Weaver, who had gone hitless, mumbled... "I'm sorry. I never swung a wood bat before."

Cookie Calaboosa said, "I'd renounce baseball, but, at this time in my life, it's all I want to do."

Iggy Fanoki took me aside. "Mister McKay, I can't play no more. I forgot how."

"You have amnesia?"

"Yeah, that's what I got."

"Then how do you know who I am?" I asked.

He paused, then said, "I got part-time amnesia. It comes and goes and I can never tell when."

"Iggy," I leveled, "why are you afraid to go out there and play?"

"I ain't afraid, I'm just nervous, my hair's fallin' out, I'll be older than shit before my next birthday."

"Iggy," I sagely advised, "there's plenty of time to be older than shit later in life. Right now, appreciate the fact that you're talented. Trust your ability to perform. If you didn't believe in yourself you wouldn't be here, would you?"

Iggy nodded. Something got through.

As the boys left the clubhouse I noticed Duke Rudolf was still walking with a pronounced limp. I asked, "Everything okay?"

"Charley horse, nothing serious," he said, hobbling off.

I heard a woman's voice behind me. "It's more than a charley horse."

I turned to this pint-sized, elderly woman with a welcoming face that made me smile. She wore a hunting cap, bib overalls, a Colt forty-five holstered to her hip, carried a medical bag.

"So you're our new general manager," she said with a soothing lilt to her voice. She handed me a sheet of paper. "Here is the injury report. Duke Rudolf has a mild strain in his left hip flexor muscle. Streamline West has a strained right shoulder. Stubby Jenks is suffering from recurring back spasms. Scraps Wisenheimer is experiencing migraines. Rabbi Melman took a foul ball off his left toe and can't get his shoe on. Noodles Weaver tweaked his left hamstring, I told him to sit out for a few days and he agreed, but his father insists that he play. I tried talking to manager Pratt and I couldn't understand a word the man said, so what are you going to do about it?"

I paused to absorb this. "Have we been introduced?"

"Oh, goodness gracious me, I'm forgetting my manners," she said, clasping my hand in hers. "Doctor Edna Squeamish. That RV parked outside is my infirmary. Where I care for my boys. My children. My late husband, Swede, and I never had children. The boys call me 'Mom'. I hope you will, too."

I pointed to her Colt 45. "Never refuse a mother with a gun."

"Oh, this thing doesn't work," she gaily laughed. "In Clowntown it's all about fashion."

Ralph Dalton Futz called with his latest scoop. "My extensive research has unearthed a nugget that may interest you. After poring over rivers of sports columns, circa nineteen-sixties, I have brought this item to light… It seems that Heinie Pratt and Tinky Farzock, although members of opposing teams, were the best of friends off the field…Enter Rosarita, the Latino spitfire, who captured both their hearts. What resulted was a feud between the two men that included public slurs, physical altercations, even death threats. Rosarita, the woman in question, dumped both men, married a British Lord and became a Lady. My invaluable time will be affixed to your account."

CHAPTER TWENTY

My boys are keeping late hours. It's affecting their game. I'm going to have to lay down the law and declare the Animal Bar off-limits. I'm sure Clowntown has more to offer in the way of entertainment. Stuff like bowling, a haircut, watching a haircut, watching a bowler get a haircut...

...Then again, there's Tempest. The woman intrigues me, stimulates my wild side. I might stop by. See her again. It's been a while since I was in a relationship with a woman, and I'd be married right now if she hadn't met that rich guy.

"*Boom-thumpa-boom!*"

I flashed my ID to Max Doody.

The Schnitzel Sisters (Brunhilda & Brunhelga) danced around me twirling their tassels with verve and vivation!

Destiny, covered in balloons, passed out pins for pricking.

Chastity did push-ups on Duke's lap.

Allstate and Cloris, the bow-legged contortionist, simulated sex on the dance floor.

Luscious led Heinie into a back room marked *Paradise*.

Stubby was engrossed in a comic book.

Noodles tried to get the claw to pick up the stuffed monkey.

Iggy was losing at craps.

I was greeted by the nasally-pinched voice of Mayor Mongrel J. Clown. "Ah, Mister McKay, welcome to my noble establishment. Tonight's special—five bucks off the missionary position."

"No, thanks," I replied. "Just dropped by to meditate."

The Mayor failed to see the humor, so I moved things forward by asking, "Don't you think owning a brothel might tarnish your reputation?"

"Who needs a reputation," he answered, "I own this town. And I've got big plans, tremendous plans. Gonna build a second floor, add more rooms, waterbeds, a gift shop. Sell wet t-shirts, used g-strings, fuck videos, a real high-end operation."

There was a loud commotion as Tempest rocketed a man headfirst out the front door, yelling—*"Come in here again you'll find your head up your ass!"*

She marched back behind the bar. I took a stool and remarked, "Quiet night, huh?"

"The usual hullabaloo," she said, flashing me a lusty smile. "Glad you could join us."

"Couldn't resist."

"What'll you have?"

"Pabst Blue Ribbon."

Tempest went to fetch my PBR. I tried to think of something clever to say when she returned and the best I came up with was…"What's a nice woman like you doing in a place like this?"

"Bullfighting," she said plunking down my beer. "If there's anything else you need be sure to let me know."

"Yes. Yes, there is," I said, "I was wondering if I could treat you to lunch sometime?"

"Most guys want breakfast."

"I'd like to get to know you."

"Better not ask me out," she warned. "My ex-husband won't like it."

"What's your ex-husband got to do with it?"

"Ask him," she pointed, "he's sitting right next to you."

Tempest hurried back to work, and there he was, a couple hundred pounds with greasy hair, squinty eyes, a cigarillo dangling from his thick lips. I was especially aware of the AK-47 in his grasp.

I forced a friendly grin and said, "Y'think the Packers'll go all the way this year?"

"What the fuck you up to?" he sneered through rusty teeth.

"Trouble I'm guessing."

"Leave my wife alone."

"You mean ex-wife."

"Tempest belongs to me."

"You don't *own* her."

"How about me and my friends educate ya?" he said, suddenly flanked by a trio of bumpkin buddies.

"You need *help*?" I foolishly mocked. "You scared to take me on alone?"

"Step outside and see how scared I am," he challenged.

"You talk big for a guy with a gun."

He slammed his AK-47 on the bar. "My fists'll do the talkin'."

Tempest appeared, glared at her former spouse—"Okay, Royal, knock off the bully bit."

She turned to me. "Royal can't get it through his head that we're divorced."

"You ain't goin' out with this dip," Royal commanded.

"It's my life," she insisted, "and If I want to go out with this dip I will go out with this dip."

Tempest threw her arms around me and said, "Springer, darling, I accept your invitation for breakfast."

"Breakfast...?" I sputtered.

Royal picked up his weapon, pointed it at me and snarled, "Next time I see ya, you'll have holes in yer head."

CHAPTER TWENTY ONE

The boys' clubhouse topic was sexual conquests with points scored. First base is kissing, second base is feeling one boob, third base is a two-boober, sliding home wins a game they call *Pussy Pong*.

Once the game was over, with no credible winner, Ron Rigler asked Noodles Weaver, "How come I never see you with a girl?"

"Just shy I guess," Noodles offered in his defense.

"I'm thinking you're a Tinkerbell," taunted Rigler.

"I'm not gay."

"Then it's time for you to prove it. I'll fix you up with the Schnitzel Sisters, they're having a two-for-one sale."

"Oh, no," Noodles wavered, "I couldn't…"

"Okay," Rigler persisted, "how about the ever-popular—Cricket Monsoon!"

"Yeah," Scraps approved. "She's built like a brick tit house."

Noodles gulped. "No, I could never…"

"Why not?" Rigler prodded. "Is it because you're a bumfucker?"

"I'm as straight as anybody else," Noodles stated.

"Great," smirked Rigler. "I'll split for the cash. It's a charitable donation."

"Pssssst!" Leo motioned for me to join him and, in a shaken voice, he said, "My life is an emotional tilt-a-whirl."

"Rub some dirt on it."

"It won't help," he whined. "If we don't start winning we'll have to shut down."

"We're not shutting down, Leo. The team is improving. We're losing by less. Have faith. Things'll turn around."

"Yeah, sure," he shrugged, "but while we're waiting to have faith we need to get fans in the park, so I'd like to bounce some ideas off of you."

"Bounce away," I said.

"Okay, how about this? We'll paint our hot dogs green and tell the fans to use them as a hex against the opposing team. With everybody waving their green weenies it should be quite a sight."

"What's the next idea?"

"Between innings we'll have Allstate Cabrera race a horse."

"And Allstate breaks a leg and has to be shot."

"Oh…Okay, how about this? A Civil War reenactment!"

"Tell me you're out of your mind."

"No! They use *real* bullets."

"What's the next idea?"

"You're gonna love this one," Leo forged on. "We announce that someone on the team killed Nutty and we'll take a poll and the fans will be judges and decide who did it."

Time to nip this in the bud. "Leo, mi amigo, your brain has been hijacked by network TV. If we want the fans to come we have to put our efforts into motivating our players. Right now, they go out there thinking they're going to lose. What's needed is an attitude adjustment. Maybe if we got ourselves affiliated with a Major League organization the boys would feel they have a future. Something to shoot for."

A smile painted Leo's lips. "So you know," he said.

"Know what?"

"Well, old pal, it just so happens I seized the initiative and have been in direct contact with the *Chicago Cubs*. Talked to the head *Cub* himself, and he might be more than interested in having the *Clowntown Clowns* become part of his organization."

"You're making this up."

"I wanted it to be a surprise. So—*surprise!*"

"You're making this up."

"Have faith, partner, my *Clowns* are going places!"

I was calling Ralph Dalton Futz when a call came in from Ralph Dalton Futz. The man claims to have supernatural powers. This is one of them. "Springer, dear fellow," he began, "I have conducted an extensive background check on your Mister Pratt and here is what I have brought to light…It seems that Heinrich Hugo Pratt spent five years in a mental institution. While incarcerated, he was accused of murdering his roommate. His guilt was never proven. Nor his innocence. Baseball banned him for life."

CHAPTER TWENTY TWO

A doubleheader versus the *West Sweden Sturgeons*. Before game one Heinie gave another one of his loose-leaf pep talks, ending with, "I've seen worse teams than us and most even better, so we better be better cuz we're goin' against Tricky Nickels who throws lightnin' from his right and from his left cuz he's bi-sexual, so get out there and kick his butt."

The team trudged out of the clubhouse, ready to have their butts kicked.

Leo jumped forward and shouted—"*Everybody stop!* I have breaking news! It just so happens Mister McKay and I have been contacted by the *Chicago Cubs* and they're sending a scout to look us over. He should be here any day now."

We kicked *Sturgeon* butt in both games!

Virgil Weathers notched a win in game one. Scraps Wisenheimer went five-for-five. Cookie Calaboosa, who socked two homers and knocked in six runs, told me, "This morning, I saw Jesus in my pancakes."

Streamline West tossed a second game shutout. Ron Rigler closed the ninth. Noodles Weaver homered in the winning runs. Cookie made three defensive gems at first base because, "God was in my glove."

The *Clowntown Clowns* are on a roll! Eight straight wins! Spirits are high. Heinie refuses to take off his uniform. To wash it is bad luck. To smell it is worse.

After close observation I am finding that Heinie Pratt is far from the hero I used to worship. I see an embittered man. Angry. Confused. A loose cannon. Just how loose is up for grabs. When I asked him if he knew Tinky Farzock was a clown he evaded the question, said *everyone's* a clown in his book. But he knew Tinky Farzock. He hated Tinky Farzock. Threatened to kill Tinky Farzock.

A prime suspect if I ever saw one.

I knew Leo hadn't contacted the *Chicago Cubs*, but it seemed like a terrific idea so I called and left a message for *Cubs'* general manager, Ernie Wacker. Then another message. So far I'm oh-for-five. Make that six. Never say never. Maybe I'll see Jesus in my pancakes.

Today's game with the *Dead Lake Loons* was rained out.

I made another call to Ernie Wacker and, when he actually answered, there was a knock at my door.

There stood Tempest in a drippy slicker. "Ready for breakfast?" she asked.

I told Wacker I'd call him back.

When Tempest said breakfast she meant breakfast which is how we found ourselves ensconced in a greasy spoon called *The Pork & Cheese*.

I opened with, "You from around here?"

"Born and bred in the woods," she replied.

"Animal Bar...work there long?"

"I know what you're thinking," she said, "it's a whore house. The girls are prostitutes. Well, just because they're great in bed doesn't make them bad people. These are young women trying to survive in this Godforsaken community. When they earn enough money, they'll go out and make a difference in the world. Some of the girls have done it. We have a graduating class of three lawyers, a judge, and the lieutenant governor of a very large state."

Tempest asked about me, so I filled her in. Comedy writer. Lucky to be in the joke business. Humor has the power to heal. Stuff like that.

"Tempest what?" I inquired. "I never got your last name."

"Bedwedder," she said, "I'm Danish. I was a Jensen before I was a Bedwedder."

"Then Billie is your daughter?" I surmised.

She beamed. "Oh, you've met my little over-achiever."

"Could be the next Sandy Koufax."

"She's no stick in the woods," Tempest asserted. "My Billie's gonna amount to something...Me, I got knocked up. Had to get married. It's what bad teenaged girls did to become good teenaged girls. I was sixteen, didn't know shit about being a wife. The most important decision in my life and I was clueless."

She continued. "Me and Royal had a give and take relationship at first. Then, after a couple of months of bliss, he became controlling. I was always apologizing for something he did, like it was my fault. I was losing who I am. So, after too many lost years hoping he would change, I divorced him. Now I'm moving on, and just because we live in the same house doesn't give Royal the right to supervise my life."

I did a triple-take. "You and Royal *live* together...?"

I was smacked in the head with a wadded-up napkin.

In a booth across the room sat Royal Bedwedder, itching for a showdown.

CHAPTER TWENTY THREE

Got through to *Cubs'* general manager, Ernie Wacker, introduced myself and launched into a sales pitch explaining how the *Clowntown Clowns* are on fire—lots of talent—loads of prospects to be prospected…

Wacker interrupted. "You're wasting your time, McKay, I get calls all the time from low-level teams like yours."

"We're not low-level. We're professional ballplayers and we deserve to be treated as such."

"If you're professionals how come I never heard of you?"

"Because we're the best kept secret in baseball."

"Let me know when you're not," he laughed as he clicked off.

"Well, that was uncalled for," I grumbled to myself, going on to vow—"I am not letting one little rejection stop me. I will not let my boys down. Wacker hasn't heard the last of Springer McKay."

Before today's game against the *Beaverbrook Bullheads*, a dark cloud rose up over the stadium. A mayfly invasion. Mayflies in August. They must have overslept.

Max Doody ambled up and said, "Those mayflies are very athletic. Have sex flyin' through the air. Wish I had wings."

The exhausted mayflies closed their show. The game got underway.

Bottom of the first, Scraps Wisenheimer got hit in the head by a pitch. The Mayor called the pitch a strike. Scraps picked himself off the ground, clouted the Mayor in the nose, the Mayor ejected Scraps, but we managed to squeak by the *Bullheads* 2-0 extending our win streak to nine games.

Doc Squeamish told Heinie and me that Scraps had suffered a concussion. "The boy thinks it's 'sissy' to wear a helmet," she said. "As a result he is delirious and cannot count past three. I recommend he rest for several weeks so I can monitor his behavior."

Heinie wouldn't have it. He wasn't about to lose his slick second baseman because of some ball to the head. "I got balls to the head all the time," he said, "and I came out okay cuz in my day men were tough and got off the mat to get hit again, and they're all dead now, but that's the chance they took."

Doc Squeamish continued to argue her case, citing the dangers of mistreated injuries, and she might have changed Heinie's mind if she hadn't called him a pig-headed twit.

I know Scraps was asking for it, crowding the plate like he always does, but these bad calls by the Mayor are killing us. It's like he's doing it on purpose.

The Mayor's office was at the First Clown Security Integrity Fidelity Bank & Trust Company. A huge sign on his office door read —

MAYOR MONGREL J. CLOWN
CEO
President
Notary Public

The Mayor's pink-headed secretary was wearing so much mascara her eyes were missing. The floppy-eared nameplate on her desk told me her name was Bunny.

"Hey there, Bunny," I greeted, "Springer McKay to see the Mayor."

She stabbed her intercom with a purple nail. "Mister Mayor, your honor, sir," she squeaked, "there's a Sprinkler McCray to see you…"

She doled out a vacant smile. "He says go in."

Mayor Clown's office was cheaply furnished with timberland closeouts. The walls were crammed with framed awards for everything. An entire stuffed moose took up a good portion of the room. An antler almost put my eye out.

The Mayor was seated in a grandly indulgent throne. He wore a bandage on his pointy nose. Looked like a shady Pinocchio.

"Bunny's quite a treat, isn't she?" he smirked.

"She carries herself well."

"Are you kidding? She blows my mind…and a whole lot more, if you catch my drift."

"I'm afraid I do."

The Mayor gestured to a chair. "Sit down, sit down, make yourself comfy."

It was hard, wooden, hemorrhoid hell.

The Mayor fired-up a cigar. "So what brings a well-heeled Hollywood person like you to my humble counting house? Wait, don't tell me, you want to open an account. We'll start with, let's say, four million?"

"I'm not here to open an account."

"You'll get a free ballpoint pen."

"I was hoping for a toaster."

The Mayor didn't get it, pasted me a dead-level look. "McKay, there's something we need to talk about."

"Yes, about your umpiring…"

He waved off the idea. "No, no, what I have to discuss is of much greater importance." He paused for effect…"Would you entertain the idea of selling Clowntown Memorial Stadium? I mean, I wouldn't blame you if you did. it's over one-hundred years old, a decaying fragment, a blotch on the proud name of Clowntown."

"You should be talking to Leo," I said. "He owns the fragmented blotch."

"Yes I know" the Mayor cringed. "But every time I try to talk to him he runs away and since he won't speak to me I'm sure you can speak for him."

"I don't think Leo wants to sell the ballpark."

"Why not?"

"Because I don't want him to."

The Mayor turned a beety red. "Look, McKay, get smart, unload the damn thing. The former owner wasn't smart, wouldn't sell to me, ran off with my wife, but that's not important right now."…He paused to unclench his jaw, then said, "Look, I'll be honest with you."

"That would be nice."

"You see, the truth is, I have a fantastic idea that will boost the economy of my beloved Clowntown."

I strung him along. "A fantastic idea? Wow. Care to tell me about it?"

"Of course, if you insist." He gazed off…"Picture this. The Mongrel J. Clown Memorial Flea Market! Millions of customers in acres of tents. Hundreds of vendors selling crap you never knew you wanted. It will be a tourist destination. Put my town on the map. So, go consult with your Mister Merkin. Impress upon him the urgency of selling while he can. To be quite honest, your ballpark is crumbling, unsafe, there's no telling what might happen."

When I left the bank I checked to see if my wallet was still there, and imagine my surprise when it was.

I don't trust this phoney baloney Mayor. What's he up to? How much profit is there in tube socks?

CHAPTER TWENTY FOUR

Got to the ballpark early the next day, headed to my office in the press box. No press box. Vanished overnight.

Leo rushed up, saying, "What the heck happened? It's like a tornado chopped it off! There's lumber all over the field!"

"This was no tornado, Leo," I said. "It was Mayor Clown. I expected vandalism to be rats in the wiener water, but never this."

"What'll we do?" Leo asked in a frenzy.

"You said you wanted a new ballpark."

"That would cost millions."

"You can afford it."

"Of course I can. Better yet, we'll threaten to move the team and the fans will pay for a new park."

"They'll think it's a tax and shoot us."

"Yeah," Leo sighed, "what choice would they have?"

"All right," I said, "time for show and tell. Exactly how much money do you have?"

"It's a tidy sum."

"I know it's tidy. How tidy? I want a number."

"I'm not very good at numbers," Leo admitted, "that's why I hired Skeets Jaggler. Big wealth manager in L. A. He only charges a twenty-six percent commission. Most of them charge twenty-seven. I'll have him send you my numbers."

I wasn't about to wait for Skeet's numbers, so I got Skeet's number off his website and called L.A. to learn the meaning of the word "tidy."

A woman's voice repeatedly informed me my call was very important…Twenty minutes later I doubted her sincerity and hung up.

Noodles Weaver's locker was festooned with condom balloons.

Ron Rigler placed a baseball bat in Noodles' hands, saying, "It is with great honor that I hereby present you with the Peter Prick award for outstanding fornication. Today you are a man."

The boys hoot-hooted their applause, urged Noodles to tell them all about it and don't leave anything out!

"Well, first I introduced myself to Cricket," he began, "and we talked and she's really not cheap like on the outside. Inside she's smart and funny and so am I she thinks. Then I gave her money and she took me in the back and I never heard a girl scream *'Fuck me, caveman!'* before."

"Yeah, yeah, what else?" Iggy was panting to know.

"Her boobs are like rocks, she must work out a lot."

"Don't stop now," urged Scraps, "Junior's about to blow!"

"What can I say, guys," Noodles shrugged, "I'm in love."

A stupefied silence.

Streamline was the first to speak. "Interesting," he said. "Are you referring to love in the romantic sense?"

"I sure am."

"Oh, c'mon," said Duke, "guys don't get serious about girls like her."

"She has a reputation," warned Rabbi Melman.

"A fallen woman," added Cookie.

"But I'm in *love*," Noodles declared.

"People get over that," said Iggy.

Noodles shook his head. "Not me. I'm a for-keeps kind'a guy."

"Go ahead," chided Scraps, "tie yourself down, let some broad walk all over ya, see if I give a shit."

"I would never let woman walk all over me," said Rigler. "Unless, of course, she's into that sort of thing."

"Take it from one who knows," offered Coach Doody, "you get attached to a woman, you get pussy-whipped."

"Wait a minute," said Virgil, "I'm a married man and I'm not pussy-whipped."

This ignited a debate on pussy-whipping.

...But Noodles wasn't listening. "I hit for the cycle after I slept with her," he told me. "Cricket's good luck and I'll have to sleep with her before every game even if it blows my savings. It would be bad luck not to."

The boys moved on to a game called "What's your favorite thing about a girl?" Among the replies were big knockers, perky jugs, huge bazooms, golden bozos and Egyptian water carriers.

Nine-year-old Peewee joined in to say, "Sure can't wait till I can touch a perky jug."

Doctor Edna Squeamish, standing in the doorway, addressed the group. "I have been observing you boys for some time now, and I am hoping to hear a conversation that does not involve the female anatomy. If you ever expect to be honest-to-goodness men you will have to get over this inane concept of man as hunter and woman as prey. It closes the mind. Makes you ignorant. And if you insist on being ignorant I will refuse to do your laundry and you will play in poopy pants."

CHAPTER TWENTY FIVE

Sheriff Clowndale paid a call. "I did some background checks on your team," he chirped. "Didn't turn up a whole lot till I got to Cookie Calaboosa. Turns out the kid has a record. In and out of jail for shoplifting, drinking, fighting, working his way to a felony. Last report, he ran away from home. Seems like a nice kid, but looks can be deceiving."

Cookie didn't deny the background check, admitted he'd been a rotten apple. But he didn't run away from home, his parents ran away from him. He came home one night to find they had moved out. He took shelter in the nearby church. The congregation helped him find God and God found him a home in baseball. "Glory be to God."

During today's game against the *Timberville Splinters* Max Doody came to me with a request. "I want Warren Weaver out'a this dugout," he grumped. "Look at him over there givin' Noodles battin' advice. That's my job. It's a "historical" baseball rule—no civilians on the bench."

I approached Warren, asked him to leave the dugout. Warren insisted his boy needed him. I told him I was sorry and explained the "historical" rule. When Warren refused to budge Noodles walked up to his father and said, "Mister McKay's the boss, dad, I think you better leave."

Noodles walked off. Warren turned to me and laid down the law. "My boy says he likes you, even trusts you, so keep him away from that bitch he thinks he's in love with. Noodles and me have a plan and him getting hooked up with some cheap tramp is not part of it."

Warren shouted over to Noodles—"Its okay, son, I'll be right behind the dugout."

We notched our tenth victory in a row clobbering the *Splinters* by a score of 12-0. Virgil Weathers pitched a complete game. Noodles batted in six runs without the advice of his dad who was now giving batting tips to Peewee.

The *Clown* players had witnessed the incident with Noodles and his father. They all had something to say about it.

"That was really neat, the way you stood up to your dad," Iggy told Noodles. "I never stood up to my dad. He left home when I was two."

"Dad means well," Noodles explained. "He wants me to have what he never got and he gets pretty emotional about it."

"My father is overflowing with emotion," offered Rabbi Melman. "A sensitive, loving man who I am not afraid to hug."

"My father never hugged," said Cookie. "He said it made him look weak."

"Dad and me are best buds," Streamline chimed in. "He's always there to support me."

"Lucky you," drawled Virgil. "Paw told me I didn't have a chance in baseball. But then, he never did hold a job for long."

"I hardly knew my old man," Stubby disclosed. "He never took the time to raise me."

"I never knew my dad," murmured Scraps. "He died before I was born."

"One time pop broke my arm when we were wrestling," Duke recalled. "He did it on purpose. He was losing."

"That's nothing," Rigler joined in. "Father insisted on interviewing all the fabulous babes I was dating. Then he ran away with one."

Allstate rattled off something, Duke translated..."He says, 'My father and I never spoke. He was Polish and didn't speak Spanish'."

I celebrated our victory at the Big Rack Lounge indulging myself in one of th*eir* special old-fashioneds. Instead of olives, Spike Clownhowser garnishes with chili peppers. Following CPR it's surprisingly refreshing.

It was impossible not to notice Mayor Mongrel J. Clown was holding an election rally. Armed yokels cheered his speech. The joint rocked when he raised his rifle and invoked the name of God eight or nine times. He crammed in lines like—*"I will continue to fight for you." "We will go forward together." "Vote for me and you'll be so happy you won't believe it!"*

Hard to argue with that last one.

Sheriff Clowndale slipped onto the stool next to me and said, "Your team is starting to show some life. Me and the wife are going to the games again."

"Yeah," I acknowledged. "all of a sudden my team is popular. The local paper is doing a feature on us, the boys will be signing autographs at the *Clown Car Company*, and we've been invited to a *Meet the Players* event where I will have the honor of crowning the Kraut Queen while a chorus of cheeseheads do the hand jive."

"I know," smiled the Sheriff. "I'm a cheesehead."

The yokels began to march single-file around the room, weapons held high, as they chanted—*"Win with Mongrel Clown, he never let us down. He'll cut our taxes with his axes, never frown with Clown!"*

They formed a conga line and floundered out the door.

"Look at those people," said the Sheriff. "A flock of robots. They keep re-electing him because he tells them what they want to hear, even if they don't know what they want to hear until he tells them what he wants them to hear whether it's true or not. But enough about that skunk. What's new with the Nuckleball case? What have you got so far?"

I knew the Sheriff wouldn't believe me if I kept my mouth shut, so I said—"Well, I'm gathering my thoughts, have a few theories, spitballs in the air, nothing concrete…"

"You don't know shit," the Sheriff deduced.

"That's one way to put it," I nodded.

"What's say we review what we got so far," he said, snatching up a napkin and jotting…"The *Clowntown Clowns* have eleven players, one manager, two coaches, that mysterious owner, one batboy and you. That's a total of seventeen people in the dugout at the exact moment of the crime. Seventeen suspects."

"Make that eighteen," I noted. "Warren Weaver."

"How about I haul them all in for questioning?"

"No," I cautioned, "that might scare off the culprit, and I've got to keep this team together."

My boys are restless. When's this *Chicago Cub* scout gonna show up?

In desperation, I left a message for Ernie Wacker, said I was calling from the Commissioner of Baseball's office and would he please contact me at once.

Wacker promptly returned my call and didn't seem thrilled to be talking to me again. I insisted he let me have my say. The *Clowntown Clowns* are hot. Ten straight wins. Burning up the *Northwoods League*. The *St. Louis Cardinals* might be sending a scout, but I'm a long-time *Cub* fan and I'd like to give him first crack at us.

Wacker said not to make a move until he gets back to me.

CHAPTER TWENTY SIX

Today, we embark on a five-hour trek to *Musty Valley* for a three-game set against the *Flying Squirr*els. An enthusiastic crowd of yokels were gathered around the lopsided school bus cheering on their winning team!

Old Bob Snooks came up, did a couple of practice swings with his hefty bat. "How about takin' me along, McKay?" he said. "I have the power of ten men."

To which I replied, "Can't fit 'em in, Bob, the bus is full up."

"Then put me in with the luggage."

"Look, Bob," I said, "when I need you, you'll be the first to know."

"It would be a smart move," he nodded. "I'm an offensive threat."

I noticed Billie Bedwedder sneaking on the bus. "Hey. where do you think you're going?"

"On the trip," she smiled, pounding a ball in her glove. "I'm not too young. One time, in an exhibition game, this teenaged girl, Jackie Mitchell, struck out Babe Ruth and Lou Gehrig."

"Yeah, that's a fact," I nodded…"Look, Billie, you have talent, there's no doubt about that, and I'm sure it won't be long until you get the chance."

She ran off in tears, saying, "You're nothing but a sexual supremacist misanthrope!"

Mayor Clown made a grand entrance, accompanied by six cheerleaders twisting their bodies to spell —

C-L-O-W-N-S

Not an easy thing to do.

The Mayor took his place behind the podium, switched the microphone ON and bellowed to the yokels—"My friends! And you *are* my friends because nobody tells me who my friends are. It is a great, great honor and fantastic privilege for me to wish our very amazing *Clowns* incredible success on their tremendous journey because God is on their side, and on my side, and I am on your side in this great country I like to call America!" He pumped his fist in the air and shouted—"Go Clowns, go!"

The yokels screeched as one—"*Go Clowns, go! Go Clowns go! Go Clowns go!*"

"And thank you in advance for your vote," the Mayor concluded, switching *OFF* the microphone.

I joined the Mayor at the podium. "Hey, your honor. Nice of you to show your support. I was beginning to think you didn't like us."

The Mayor waved away the suggestion, a sign a lie was on its way, so I switched *ON* the microphone.

"Was there ever any question?" he said. "I've been a *Clown* supporter in the very best of times and the very worst of times, and not for an instant have I wavered in my unbelievable loyalty. Our *Clowns* represent the very finest Clowntown has to offer and if there is anything, anything at all that I can do for our team don't be afraid to ask."

"Well, the ballpark is a decaying fragment," I said for all to hear. "How about you restore Clowntown Memorial Stadium to its former glory?"

"Yes, of course, most certainly," he instantly replied. "We must do all we can to help our boys in uniform."

"And Mongrel J. Clown is a man who keeps his promises. Right, your honor?"

"I am a man of my word."

The yokels cheered the Mayor! The Mayor's face pocked purple as he realized the microphone was *ON*. He quickly switched it *OFF* and took refuge in his Lexus.

I saw Tempest Bedwedder coming toward me. She looked smashing in a work shirt tied at the waist. Her button was an inny. Red hair framed her shoulders with fiery beauty. Think Maureen O'Hara in *The Quiet Man* or Rita Hayworth in anything.

"Hey, Springer," she smiled. "You haven't been at the Animal Bar lately. I've missed you."

"Been working," I explained. "The *Chicago Cubs* may be sending a scout to look us over."

"Well, try to find time to look me over," she said, planting me a kiss that steamed my shorts.

Over Tempest's shoulder, I could see Royal Bedwedder, glaring at me, twirling his shotgun like a baton.

CHAPTER TWENTY SEVEN

Our bus hiccupped its way to *Musty Valley*. A pinheaded old codger named "Grinny" was hunched in the drivers' seat, piloting the *Starship Enterprise as he* blabbered—*"We need more power, Captain!"*…*"I'm a doctor, Jim, not a dancer!"*…*"Tribbles to the left, Tribbles to the right, Tribbles in my hair, TrIbbles everywhere…"*

I took a seat next to Leo. He turned to me and moaned, "I get bus sick."

I shoved his head out the window in the nick of time.

The bus was hot, sweaty, I know how a roast chicken feels. Not that my boys were bothered. Since Doc Squeamish wasn't around to hear, they were engaged in a bragging competition.

"The snatch is throwin' themselves at me," boasted Scraps.

"I'm havin' sex with chicks I hardly met," Iggy blustered.

"I had five babes at an orgy," gloated Rigler.

"I can't wait to get my snatch at an orgy," Peewee chipped in.

The sex talk petered out so to speak. The boys settled in for cards, thumbing phones, picking noses. Rigler filed his nails to sharp points. Rabbi Melman pored over his Torah Cliff Notes.

Stubby's froggy voice burst out with —"One-hundred bottles of beer on the wall, one-hundred bottles of beer…!"

He was pelted by baseball mitts.

Iggy and Scraps were playing poker in the seats behind me. "That's five bucks you owe me," said Scraps. "Cough it up."

"Can't," sighed Iggy. "I'm busted."

"You're stupid," said Scraps.

"You're stupider."

"You're dumb."

"You're dumber."

Tuning out this high-level banter I glanced over at Cookie Calaboosa, his cherubic face buried in his Bible.

"I know how it ends," I said. "The devil did it."

Cookie looked up with a contented smile. "The Good Book deepens my faith, Mister McKay. All I want in life is to set a good example and improve the human condition."

"It could use a tune-up."

"I'm attending Saint Mickeys, an all-night church in Clowntown," he continued. "Except I don't think there ever was a Saint Mickey. He's not in the Bible, even though I have hard time believing everything in the Bible. Not that I'm being critical, God forbid, but it's hard for me to accept the fact that the Bible is the complete and perfect word of the Lord. I mean, there are experts who say the Bible has been rewritten and even parts cut out. Do you think that's true?"

"I'm a writer. I cut and rewrite all the time."

"It sure makes a person wonder," Cookie went on. "Like the story of Noah's Ark. I mean, c'mon, *two* of each? He would've had to build a Norwegian cruise ship. And how can a virgin have a baby?"

"Virgin was a name for a young woman," I said.

"So Joseph really knocked her up?"

"In the biblical sense."

We were interrupted by Allstate Cabrera, sharpening his skills by sliding headfirst down the aisle. He stood up and shouted—*"Seguro!"* (Spanish for *"Safe!"*)

Allstate kept this up for a total of twelve stolen bases until his teammates blocked the aisle, shouting—*"Fuera!"* (Spanish for *"Out!"*) Allstate retired to his seat, saying, *"Motherfuck!"* (English for *"Motherfuck!"*)

My nose wafted to the whiff of ancient China. The source was Duke Rudolf, slathering a salve on himself. "Don't you just love that smell?" he said. "Tiger Balm. Works wherever it hurts."

"Smells like you hurt all over."

"No, I'm feeling great," he assured me. "Just some soreness from when I dove in the stands for that liner. The guys kid me about being accident prone, but I'd like to see them stop rockets at third."

"I know what you mean." I said. "I played third base in the sixth grade. The first game I made five errors and got traded to kindergarten for a child to be named later."

Duke chuckled. "Good, that's good…Look, I know what you came here to say. I should stop trying to organize the guys. You don't want a union even though they need one. Well, let me educate you. These guys work hard. They're doing the job, providing entertainment, they deserve a living wage. Dad, Gramps, Uncle Goofy, they were all union. I couldn't have become a lawyer without their savings and support."

"If you're a lawyer why aren't you lawyering?" seemed the logical thing to ask.

"All in good time," Duke explained. "But, first, I have something to prove. I'm a good ballplayer. With any luck I'll make big bucks in the majors. Then I'll retire, open my own law firm, and continue to advocate for the disadvantaged."

I felt the *sting* of a pea on the back of my neck! Turned to see the shooter was Iggy Fanoki, pea shooter dangling from his mouth, pretending to be asleep.

I leaned close to him and whispered, "Iggy, I know you're awake."

His eyes popped open. "Then could you lend me a hundred bucks?"

"What for?"

"'Cause I need money."

"Why is that?"

"Those crap games at the Animal Bar. I know I can win big, but the guys won't lend me more dough."

"Iggy," I cautioned, "has it occurred to you that you're throwing your money away?"

"I ain't throwin' my money away."

"Okay, you're throwing *my* money away."

"All I need is one lucky roll."

"The bartender told me the dice are loaded."

Iggy's eyebrows arched. Something clicked.

The bus rattled along, my mind turned to murder. The puncture on Nutty's neck was definitely caused by something sharp, so that leaves out a pea from a shooter. Peas don't puncture, peas bounce. And If the curare'-laced pea entered the killer's mouth before shooting the killer would be pushing up forget-me-nots.

Which brought me back to the Sheriff's theory—a poison-tipped dart. Like in the Charlie Chan movie. The kind that always came close to killing Abbott & Costello. All I have to do is find a poison-tipped dart, which may not be as easy as it sounds.

I walked down the aisle to stretch my legs. Overheard Spook Spindler in conversation with Max Doody who was busily carving a mermaid with legs.

"Yeah, I remember Tinky Farzock," Doody told Spook. "Played for *Cincinnati*. See these scars on my arm? They're from when I tagged him out at third and he *bit* me. Thought I was a sparerib. I wanted to strangle the sonofabitch."

"Yeah," Spook recalled, "Farzock was a bad egg. I was having a spectacular season until he did what he did."

Spook turned to me and asked, "You want to know what he did? Here is what he did. I'm on the mound. Farzock's on third. The batter executes a bunt. My catcher leaps for the ball, flips the ball to me covering home plate. Farzock slides in, spikes high, and slashes me across the face. Had to have my nose refurbished. I wanted to kill the bastard."

CHAPTER TWENTY EIGHT

Grinny landed the *Enterprise* at a Romulan truck stop for gas and a planetary whizz.

Scraps Wisenheimer stood at the next urinal. I asked how he felt after his beaning.

"Better than ever," he assured me. "The headaches are history."

At adjoining urinals, Max Doody was giving batting tips to Iggy Fanoki. "What you gotta do is make your mind a blank," he said.

"I do that all the time," Iggy replied.

"I know," Doody agreed, "you're very good at it. But you gotta *see* the ball. Nothin' but the ball. You wanna hit a grounder, you hit the top-third of the ball. You wanna hit a line drive, you hit the middle-third of the ball. A fly ball, the bottom-third."

"Couldn't I just swing and hope I hit it?"

"Your brain is full'a rocks, kid." Doody determined.

The boys raided the convenience store, loading up on Ho Hos, Ding Dongs, Maple Syrup Jerky, Rabbi Melman bought a family-size Doritos and a diet Coke. Ron Rigler washed down some pills with Mountain Dew. "Vitamins," he told me.

I had to admit I felt like a father who disapproves of his sons spending what little money they have on junk food. These are growing boys, they need a healthy diet. I, on the other hand, was older, so it was okay for me to wash down my jumbo cookie with a Yoo-Hoo.

Leo pulled me aside for a private confab. Told me the Musty Valley motel is overbooked, would I mind having a roommate? Not at all, I told him. I'm one of the boys now.

Hour three on the journey of the Enterprise. I was chatting with Virgil Weathers who seemed interested in my Hollywood career. "These here kids probably don't remember the TV shows you wrote," he drawled.

"It's such a comfort," I said.

"But I remember. My favorite was *The Nut Factory*. Great characters, real laughs."

"Yeah, everybody thought I was crazy to write a comedy about a mental institution. But when the focus groups identified with the characters I knew I had a hit."

There was one of those 'what to say next' pauses, until I said, "I like the way you've been tossing that knuckleball."

"Yeah, I never know where it's gonna go," he smiled, "but neither do the hitters."

"It's gonna get you back to the show," I assured him.

"Yup, it's my ticket to the future. Gotta have a future. The wife supports me and that ain't right. The husband wins the bread. That's what a man's gotta do."

Hour four of our voyage. I was admiring the knit mitten covering Noodles Weaver's bat. His bat is his business partner, has its own seat on the bus. The bat's name is Cricket.

"It took me a while to get used to a wood bat instead of aluminum," Noodles told me. "But, now, there's nothing like the crack of Cricket when I hit one out."

I noticed Warren was missing. "I see your dad didn't make the trip."

"Oh, he's following in his car," said Noodles. "Got Mister Merkin to make him Peewee's guardian on the road…So, anyway, the guys tell me you're a big-time writer. How'd you do that?"

"Easy. It only took ten years to become an overnight success."

"Well, ten years is a lifetime in baseball, I gotta move up quick. It's more important to me than ever. Can you keep a secret?"

"Sure."

"Cross your heart?"

I crossed my heart.

"And hope to die?"

"Maybe later. So what's your secret?"

"I'm getting married," he whispered. "I proposed and Cricket said yes."

I paused to input …"You and Cricket? Are you sure?"

"Sure as sure can be," Noodles grinned. "We haven't set a date yet, so please keep this between us. If the guys find out I'm getting married they'll think I'm a traitor to the masculine race."

"Marriage is a big step, Noodles. I imagine you've thought this through."

"Oh, yeah, Cricket promised to be faithful after we tie the knot."

I left Noodles in matrimonial reverie and ambled to the back of the bus. Heinie Pratt was laid out like the guest of honor at a wake. I joined him for a chat.

"Team's doing great," I began.

Heinie's eyes flipped open. "Whaddya want?"

"Well,' I explained, "we've been together for a while and we hardly know each other, so I thought this might be a chance for us to talk."

Heinie was defensive. "About what?"

"Well, your team is winning and you don't seem happy."

"It ain't gonna last," he muttered. "Nothin' never lasts."

"Look, Heinie, can I be frank with you?"

"Be anybody you want."

"I know what happened to you in the past."

He rose up. "You been snoopin' in my affairs?"

"No, I just think you're holding a lot of stuff inside, and if you feel the need to talk to someone, I'm someone."

"You a shrink?"

"I'm not a shrink."

"Good, I *hate* shrinks," Heinie grumbled, "had my fill of all that psycho-mumble-jumble. That pirate thing was a good idea."

"What pirate thing?"

"Do I have to draw you a pitcher?"

"Yes."

Heinie's veiny eyes brightened as he said, "I was in San Francisco, y'see, mindin' my own business. Didn't do nothin' nobody else wouldn't do. Anybody could go to the harbor and pretend to be a pirate. There's nothin' wrong with that."

"Not in my world."

Heinie's face illuminated as he re-created the scene. "It was down at Fishermen's Wharf, tourists jammin' the place. I snuck on a boat, put on my eye patch, hanky on my head, shinnied up the mast to the crow's nest. Then I took out my pecker, twirled it around and yelled—*Avast me hearties! Hornswaggle the jib! Stick it to the brisket!*... And these tourists were all gathered around, y'see, and I looked those sombitches right in the eye and I hollered—*Fuck off, you bilge-sucking scurvy knaves!*"

"I was three sheets to the wind at the time," Heinie explained, "but that didn't matter, it was somethin' I had to do. Didn't hurt nobody. Those people didn't have to haul me to the funny farm. Nothin' funny about it. The food tastes like worms."

"Y'know, Heinie," I said, "for the first time I understand what you're saying."

"I only use my scramble talk to get people to perk up and listen," he admitted. "I'm Heinie Pratt. I need to be listened to."

Heinie paused, eyed me like a stranger, and muttered, "Who do you think you are? Leave me alone."

CHAPTER TWENTY NINE

"Musty Valley!" Grinny bellowed. *"Home of Flying Squirrels and Saucers!"*

The Enterprise deposited the team at Frenchy's Shangri-La, not a Motel One or even a Twelve. The mattress was a war zone, the icebox puddled the floor, the toilet reeked of ancient piss...Need I go on?

Stubby Jenks entered the room, plopped down his catcher's gear on the bed and announced that we were *roomies*! "You wouldn't wanna room with Allstate," he warned. "He keeps the hot water on all night 'cause he can't sleep without humidity."

He opened the icebox, stuck his right hand on the block of ice. "This place might be a dump, but there's fresh ice everyday."

"You hurt your hand?" I asked with concern.

"I'm a catcher," said Stubby, "hurting my hand comes with the job. The worst is taking foul tips or trying to figure out where a knuckleball's gonna go. All that scrambling behind the plate could wreck my career before I have a career, and I am gonna have a career. Sure, people say I'm too short and don't have a chance at making it, but my time is coming. Yogi Berra wasn't tall. Built like a tank same as me. I saw him in a restaurant once when I was a little and he actually talked to me."

"What did Yogi say?"

"Your fly is open."

Stubby's giggle was infectious.

"But all humor aside," he said, "I just wanna thank you."

"You're welcome...For what?"

"For giving me hope," he said. "I've been a *Clown* for four years. My future had no future and I was all set to quit until I heard a *Cub* scout is coming. He is coming, ain't he?"

"That could very well be the case," I finagled.

"It's a good thing, too. Makes me feel like I have a chance. Like I'm gonna fulfill my dream."

Stubby gazed off..."I can see it now. Wrigley Field, the friendly confines, and the announcer announces—"Now catching for the *Chicago Cubs*, that sensational new discovery, Stubby Jenks! Boy, I would kill to hear that."

"I eat and sleep baseball," he went on. "Know all about the history of the game. Like, did you know, in 1914, Home Run Baker led the *American League* with only nine homers? Or did you know in the old days umpires used to ask the fans to rule on a play which is where instant replay got its start? Or did you know there used to be a rule where the batter told the pitcher where to throw the ball. Did you know that?"

"Can't say I did," I admitted. "What else don't I know?"

I never should have asked. Stubby did not come with an off-switch... "And did you know the *Dodgers* used to be called the *Bridegrooms*? And Johnny Bench could hold seven baseballs in one hand. And the *Giants* told Sandy Koufax he'd never make it to the big leagues. And if Boog Powell married Felipe Alou he'd be Boog Alou..."

The school bus chugged its way to Groper Field, named after Jack S. Groper owner of the Groper Brewing Company which closed forty years ago when Bullfrog Lager was found to contain frogs.

Groper Field is the home of the *Musty Valley Flying Squirrels*. Holds over a thousand fans. It's in top-notch condition thanks to the Amish who live in the woods.

The spacious visitors' clubhouse is paneled in the finest oak. Players shave at marble sinks. I never saw a walk-in locker before.

Rabbi Melman led us in prayer before the game. "We *Clowns*, here today, believe that our faith will guide us, our creator will reward us, and I will go four for four, amen."

Rabbi snapped his fingers and began to sing—"*Boys, boys, crazy boys, stay cool boys...*"

He was pelted by baseball mitts.

CHAPTER THIRTY

The first game with the *Flying Squirrels* was delayed. A mass of dead insects covered the field. Slimy. Stunk like fish.

All hands grabbed shovels, scooped the goop off the field and the game was about to get underway.

Max Doody meandered over, "Those bugs, those were cicadas, rhymes with tostadas. They come out'a the ground every once in a while to fornicate and die. Boy, that'd be the way to go."

I joined Spook Spindler on the sidelines, watched Streamline West warming up. Spook spit a stream of seeds and said, "These *Squirrels* lose more than they win, but they never lose with their Mexican sensation, Disney Cruz, on the mound. And guess who's on the mound? Disney Cruz."

"That would've been my guess."

Spook turned to Streamline with a last-minute piece of advice. "Don't give them anything to hit and don't walk anyone."

Streamline wound up, kicked high, *smacked* a fastball into Stubby's mitt!

"Looking sharp," I told him.

He looked at me, confidence lighting his eyes. "My arm feels great. I've got my command. I am destined to be on a box of Wheaties!"

Streamline turned confidence to Wheaties by shutting out the *Flying Squirrels* 10-0. He struck out twelve, no walks, hit the grand slam that sent Disney Cruz to the showers.

The *Clowns* were an offensive machine. Allstate stole three bases. Rabbi Melman went four for four. Noodles Weaver smacked two doubles, a triple, and a homer that punched a gaping hole in the polished maple scoreboard. Every player in the line-up had at least two hits and half of those were for extra bases.

There was a tense moment when Duke collided with Noodles going after a fly ball. Both claim to be okay, but I caught Duke hopping from the whirlpool to the sauna. When I asked him about it, he said, "Just a twinge, gone by tomorrow."

A bigger concern was Heinie Pratt. When he was introduced the fans booed him. He booed them back. The fans responded with a barrage of beer bottles. Heinie grabbed a bat and hit the bottles back at the fans. When he was ejected from the game he whipped out his pea shooter and shot peas at the umpire.

I ran out to get Heinie. He broke away, ran to the outfield, shinnied up a post, stood defiantly on top of the scoreboard, pulled down his pants...

I got to him before he exposed himself, grabbed his hand, he lost his balance and plunged us into a pile of dead cicadas.

Smelling like a sardine, I sent myself to the shower.

CHAPTER THIRTY ONE

The *Clowns* took all three games from the *Flying Squirrels*!

As the bus rattled us back to Clowntown, my boys had bright visions of their futures. "When I'm second baseman for the *Chicago Cubs*," Scraps imagined, "I'm gonna make ten-grand every time I step up to the plate."

"When I'm rich," Iggy joined in, "I'm gonna take a trip around the world, or maybe even someplace else."

"I am going to marry Bella Schnauzer," Rabbi Melman announced. "We're engaged. I'm saving myself for her."

"While she's sucking-off sailors." Rigler sniped.

Rabbi hit Rigler with the evilest eye he could summon and said—"Fudge off."

I wandered over to a seat next to Max Doody. He was whittling as usual. A woman's face.

"Nice work," I told him.

"Thanks for noticin'," he said. "This here chunk of butternut wood will soon be that ancient Greek statue, Venus de Milo. Right now, she's got no arms, and that ain't right, so I'm givin' her arms."

"The ancient Greeks will appreciate that."

Cookie let out a "squawk" and began hopping around on one foot!

I hurried over to him. "What's the matter?" Cookie plopped down in the aisle, blew on his smoking shoe.

"I gave him a hot foot," sniggered Rigler.

"It's not funny," Cookie whimpered. "I could have been engulfed in flames."

"It was only a gag, numbnuts," said Rigler.

"My nuts are not numb," Cookie pouted.

"Okay, dumbnuts," Rigler sneered with a laugh.

Cookie yelled after him—"*You can call me dumbnuts, just don't get personal!*"

"You okay, Cookie?" I asked.

"Yeah, I guess so," he moaned. "Rigler is always picking on me. Yesterday he cut the toes off my socks and put mud in my shoes."

Leo Merkin yanked me aside and urgently whispered, "You have to do something. Heinie's acting like a nutball."

"You noticed."

"I'd talk to him," said Leo, "but he scares me, so you talk to him."

I made my way to the back of the bus. Heinie was with Stubby, reminiscing…"Saw my first game in nineteen forty-seven, Ebbets Field, *Brooklyn Dodgers*, I was just a kid, but I remember those players like today was yesterday. Guys like Peewee Reese…"

"A ten-time all-star," said Stubby.

"…Pete Reiser," Heinie continued.

"Threw both right and left-handed," Stubby added.

"…And that new kid, Jackie Robinson."

"Rookie of the year."

"Don't you know it," said Heinie, "those *Brooklyn* bums were heroes for a sprout like me. Gonna get back to Brooklyn one day, take in another game, but right now I gotta take a nap." He went out like a light.

Stubby turned to me and whispered, "He's not such a bastard like he always is. Likes gabbing about the old days."

Stubby went back to his seat. I gave Heinie a poke. "Heinie, there's something we need to talk about."

"We already talked about something," he growled.

"This is something about something else."

Heinie sprung up. "If it's that thing in Cleveland, they never proved I was the father!"

"Heinie, we're all concerned about what happened at the game."

His eyes went blank…"Why? What happened? We won, didn't we? Did we win?"

"You don't remember?"

"Yeah, sure," he said, "of course I do, I remember one time back in St. Louis..."

"Heinie," I interrupted. "Do you remember today? Climbing on top of the scoreboard?"

"I remember going oh-for-four," he said, "but don't you worry, tomorrow I'll rip the cover off the ball, and whoever stole my peas better gimme my peas back or there's no tellin' what I might do!"

A call from Ernie Wacker. "Listen, McKay, I appreciate your patience and persistence and you make a good case for your team...so are the *Cardinals* still interested?"

"One might say that," I teased.

"Oh...Well, I just want you to know that the *Cubs* are very interested, Much more than the *Cardinals*, so I'm sending a scout to look you over."

I saw Jesus in my pancakes.

Got a text from Ralph Dalton Futz. An element essential to our case. Tinky Farzock had a record of domestic abuse.

CHAPTER THIRTY TWO

Our bus limped into town. Fans swarmed to greet their victorious *Clowns*. Never one to miss an opportunity, Mayor Mongrel J. Clown stood before the crowd, informing them that, as their public servant, he is there to serve them, and he plans to serve them so much they will say, "Please, your honor, stop serving, we don't need so much serving!"

He concluded by vowing to cut taxes. Whose taxes he didn't say.

I took the Mayor aside and said, "Mister Mayor, would you mind answering a question?"

He was wary. "Depends what it is…"

"I was just wondering why you take the trouble to campaign when you're running unopposed."

"It's good strategy," he replied through covetous eyes. "Reminds my followers how much they love me. It'll work in the long run. I'll be a fantastic governor."

I broke out a laugh. "Now, *that's* funny."

"Do I look like I'm joking?" he asked.

"I don't think that's possible," I said as I shuttled the conversation to—"So how are the renovations going at the ballpark? Can't wait to see how you're sprucing-up the place."

"Well, to be perfectly honest," the Mayor waffled, "I have yet to begin. It's an enormously huge undertaking. Planning, strategizing, permitting the permits, these things take time, bureaucracy knows no bounds. I am, however, willing to increase my offer to purchase the ballpark. Just tell me what you want."

"I want you to rebuild the press box you tore down."

"I did no such thing!" he stated.

"That's right, you hired goons."

"Are you accusing me of vandalism?"

"You catch on quick."

"Why would I buy a ballpark if I'm trying to tear it down?"

"You just answered your own question."

"I want that ballpark."

"You can't afford it."

"Name your price."

"Can't tell yet, it's going through the roof."

The Mayor took on a ghoulish demeanor and growled, "You got a mouth on you, McKay. You're a troublemaker and I don't allow troublemaking in my town. So no quibbling around the bush, I'll ask you one more time. What do you want for the ballpark?"

"Boardwalk and Park Place."

The Mayor steamed off.

Today, we launch a two-game homestand against the *Scum River Cavaliers* and Clown Memorial Stadium has a new addition. An organ. A local church was having a going-out-of-business sale and Leo snapped it up for a song. The organ comes with an eight-year-old prodigy named Alice Anne, whose repertoire consists of *Beethoven, Mozart* and *Mary had a Little Lamb*.

The *Clowns* took the field to *Beethoven's Sonata in F minor, Opus Two*, and we went on to shave the *Cavaliers* 2-zip.

Virgil Weathers went eight innings, giving up only three hits. Ron Rigler struck out the side in the ninth to notch another save.

The fans celebrated by firing their guns in the air! A pair of woodpeckers spiraled to earth. I am told they taste like chicken.

We swept both games from *Scum River*, putting us only two games behind our arch-rivals, the first-place *Kickapoo Hayhaulers*. Or, as my boys call them—the *Kickashit Noballers*.

I'm about to call Futz, Futz calls me, how is my investigation proceeding? I wasn't ready to tell him about Heinie, and how my prime suspect was showing signs of dementia, so I said, "I'm trying to track down the murder weapon. A dart. Searched the clubhouse, combed the whole stadium. No dart."

And Futz said, "My dear fellow, expand your horizons. It may not be a dart at all. It could very well be some *other* projectile…Oh, I do wish I could be there to solve this perfectly heinous crime for you, but I sold my latest screenplay to Paramount, and we're having meeting upon meeting to discuss changes in the script, and what was once murder in London is now spring break in Malibu. Not that I care, mind you. If the idiots think they wrote the film, the film gets made."

"*Some other projectile.*" Futz's words triggered my interest, and my search for the murder weapon brought me to a dilapidated old garage behind the outfield wall.

I entered to rat droppings, rifled through the mildewed drawers of a battered file cabinet, found shotgun shells, an axe, hunting knife, and a whoopee cushion that still works.

I opened a box marked baseballs. No baseballs. The box had a false bottom. Hidden under the false bottom was a slingshot, a couple of pea shooters and a small bag of peas. I emptied the bag. Mixed with the peas were pieces of a small glass bottle. Several of the peas had prickly points on them.

Holy crap on a cracker! I thought. Could the murder weapon be a prickly-pointed pea?

Figuring it would be wise to keep things as they were I carefully placed the peas and broken glass back in the bag, placed the bag, slingshot and pea shooters in the false bottom of the box, and left the garage, wondering… Who would file prickly points on peas?

CHAPTER THIRTY THREE

The girls were throwing a wedding shower for Cricket Monsoon. When I got to the Animal Bar they were in the midst of a game called *Pin the Dickie on the Donkey*.

Tempest Bedwedder was behind the bar entertaining the men with—"A man walks into a psychiatrist's office wearing Saran Wrap for shorts. The shrink looks at him and says, 'Well, I can clearly see your nuts'."

Heinie Pratt was in a heated argument with his fiancée, Luscious O'Boy.

She slapped his face. He turned her around, kicked her in the butt and clomped off, growling, "No wife'a mine is gonna work!"

Cricket, looking like an alluring fugitive from *The Rocky Horror Show*, sat at a corner table typing on a laptop.

"Don't you want to pin the dickie?" I asked.

She looked up with a winning smile. "Maybe later. I have to balance the books."

"I understand congratulations are in order," I said.

"Only if you mean it."

"Well," I admitted, "I do and I don't. I was taught by nuns. The Catholic dribbles out now and then... Is Cricket your real name?"

"No," she replied. "People call me Cricket because I 'chirp' when I come."

"Not that there's anything wrong with my line of work," Cricket went on to explain. "In a service-oriented society I provide a service. There was a guy in here yesterday. He's got nine kids. Said he wanted to have sex where it's safe."

She continued. "And you'd be surprised at how many guys like to be humiliated. One john likes to jack off while he gives me a botany lecture. Every day is a learning experience."

Her tone turned serious. "Noodles told me he was willing to quit baseball and work at a burger joint if that's what he has to do to support me, but I can always support him. I've got gold, diversified investments, I have earned every inch of my white wedding dress…Now, if you'll excuse me, it's back to the books."

I moseyed over to the bar. Tempest looked at me and said, "Hope it works out for those two kids. I'm a great believer in marriage, aren't you?"

"Oh sure," I replied. "Except for divorce, it's a great institution."

Tempest leaned close and whispered…"I get off at ten. Meet me at Clown Lake Beach." She brushed her lips against my cheek and zipped off to muddle an old-fashioned.

I glanced over to where Royal Bedwedder and his bumpkin buddies were playing darts. I gave him a neighborly wave. He threw a dart at me!

I came that close to being shish-ka-bobbed.

Wolfgang parked me at Clown Lake Beach. I spotted Tempest on the sand, joined her. We sat in silence, gazing at the warning sign of pollution.

Tempest spoke up. "They didn't teach sex education at Clowntown High, I had to take home economics. I can mop a floor in under a minute, but was an empty-headed dunce when it came to Royal Bedwedder. I actually thought I was in love with the guy. But was I ever in love? I don't know what love is. It has yet to plumb my depths."

She continued. "I'm sorry about the dart. Royal is very possessive. Thinks he owns me, it's a 'man' thing. When you get right down to it this whole town is a 'man' thing, boys learning about girls from other boys, and the other boys don't know shit about girls…So I would like to ask you, is it too much to dream about a partner who is actually a partner? Is it too much to want true intimacy, now and forever, and here you are."

Tempest locked her lips to mine.

Catching my breath I said, "Living with your ex-husband must have its challenges."

"Got no choice," she said, "We bought the house as an investment, the market took a dive, we owe more than it's worth. I won't leave, Royal won't leave, so we're living together till one of us can buy the other one out...It's been hard on Billie, even though she doesn't show it. Tough as nails that kid, she's going places."

"I brought ice cream," Tempest continued, taking a gallon from her cooler. "Peanut butter panic."

She dug in, licked the spoon, held it out. "Take a lick."

I licked the spoon, she licked the spoon, I licked her lick, she licked my lick...there's nothing like peanut butter panic in the moonlight.

We sat back, savoring the past hour an a half.

Tempest finally spoke. "I think I should warn you, it's time for the men's jet-ski races."

I found this hard to believe. "Men jet-skiing at night? That's crazy."

"That's Clowntown."

A platoon of jet skiers roared by soaking us in waves that would've swept us out to sea if this wasn't a lake.

I'll have sand in my ears for years.

I walked Tempest through the woods to her house. And there it stood. Once a grand Victorian mansion, now a decomposing money pit.

She glanced around to make sure no was looking, gave me a lingering good night kiss, then whispered..."I'm leaving Royal."

CHAPTER THIRTY FOUR

My *Clowns* were riding a fifteen-game winning streak. Heinie showered in full uniform after each game.

Max Doody explained. "Pratt ain't gonna take off his uniform till we lose. One time, I had a twenty-six game hittin' streak and ate nothin' but head cheese and tequila. If I hadn't almost died you'd be talkin' to a corpse."

In the clubhouse my boys were loose, joking, Rigler poured hot sauce in Cookie's jock.

Cookie was slumped at his locker trying to hold back the tears. I sat beside him and quipped, "Hot sauce isn't funny, ketchup is funny."

"Mister McKay," he sniffled, "you've got to stop Rigler from his reign of terror. Yesterday he put boogers in my Gatorade."

"I see your point," I nodded. "If he put liver in your shorts you'd be devoured by crows."

"Mister McKay," Cookie implored, "is it okay to wreak revenge?"

"I suppose revenge is wreakable in some cases," I said. "I wouldn't want liver in my shorts. Check out your Bible, it's loaded with 'eye for an eye, tooth for a tooth' stuff."

"I don't like fighting."

"Why use fists? Your head will think of something."

Cubs' general manager, Ernie Wacker was on the line, anxiously hoping we hadn't made a deal with the *St. Louis Cardinals*. I told him we're on the cusp.

"Well, forget St. Louis," Wacker said, "you are now an affiliate of the *Chicago Cubs*."

Only one thing remained—Drug tests.

Doc Squeamish surprised the players, handing out plastic cups. "Please remove the lid before you pee," she instructed, "then tightly close the lid and return the cups to me."

The players did as requested. Ron Rigler declined, saying, "I don't feel the urge to urinate at this particular moment. Later perhaps."

Doc was insistent, reminding him. "No pee-pee, no *Cubbie*." Rigler delivered his pee. Doc drove the samples over to the lab in Clam Falls, drove back the next day with the results.

The *Clowns* are clean!

I found Doc Squeamish in her RV infirmary treating Duke Rudolf who had what he called a ding in his knee. Doc's nimble fingers pressured the right points. "There you go," she said. "Nice as pie." Duke wobbled off.

"That young man has more than a ding," Doc told me. "His condition indicates a possible subluxation of the patella tendon. He needs an MRI, but I'm a country doctor. I don't have the facilities to properly care for my boys. I stress conditioning, but they still get injured because their boneheaded manager thinks playing through pain is a mark of manhood."

She engaged me with a smile. "So what can I do for you? Wait, don't tell me. You're wondering how Ronald Rigler passed the drug test."

"He didn't seem eager to participate."

"Well, sir," she said, "Ronald's pee showed no presence of drugs because it wasn't Ronald's pee, it was Peewee's pee. I know what Ronald is up to, but I want to protect him, give him a chance to see the error of his ways."

"You see," she went on, "I've had my own tussle with addiction. When Swede passed I couldn't sleep, afraid to be alone, so I purchased some pills from a Canadian pharmacy in India. Sedative hypnotics they're called. Had certain side effects. Pins and needles on the skin. Sleep-walking. I'd get up in the middle of the night and do things I didn't remember like baking brownies or raking leaves. Then, when Sheriff Clowndale caught me sleep-driving, I switched to chamomile tea and sleep like a bear."

"As for Ronald Rigler," Doc continued, "I lecture him on the evil of performance-enhancing drugs. He promises he'll quit... I want to believe he won't put himself out of the game forever."

"I'll go talk to him."

"No, Springer," she said. "I'm his doctor, he's in my care."

CHAPTER THIRTY FIVE

Before today's game against the *West Sweden Sturgeons*, Sheriff Gus Clowndale circled the ballpark handing out yard signs—*Don't be a Wuss, Vote for Gus*!

The Mayor was outraged! He charged over to me and grumbled, "The nerve of that nitwit thinking he can be Mayor. That hick who calls himself Clowndale and takes no pride in being a pure, unadulterated Clown. Thinks he can beat me. Ha! Not a chance. My people will never turn their backs on me, I'm a habit they can't shake."

We nearly lost. *West Sweden's* pitcher, Whip Frisbee, drilled Scraps in the head with a fastball. Scraps charged the mound, clobbered Frisbee with a series of blows. This ignited a bench-clearing brawl. The yokels cheered and shot their guns in the air. A drone crash-landed on the pitcher's mound. There are those who call this entertainment.

Back at the Big Rack Lounge Leo had another idea he wanted to try out on me. Something that would capitalize on the team's popularity.

"We should bring back Nutty Nuckleball," he said.

"He's dead Leo."

"We'll bring him back to life."

"Okay, I'm the mad doctor and you'll play Igor."

"I'm serious, Springer," Leo whined. "I even got Nutty's clown costume." He held it up. "They buried him in it."

"You dug up Nutty's costume?"

"Oh, I could never do that, I used a gravedigger."

"What's say we pursue this conversation at a later date."

"Fine by me. I gotta take this costume to the cleaners, it smells like crotch."

A poke in my back. The poker was Billie Bedwedder. "I've decided to apologize, Mister McKay. You're not an ignorant tool of absurdity."

"I knew that all along."

"Good. So I have a favor to ask. It's about my radio station."

"What radio station?"

"WFEM," she proudly stated. "If I can't play with the boys, I'll be their announcer. I'll set up a remote broadcast, conduct interviews, do the play- by-play. Okay with you?"

Discourage an entrepreneur? Not a chance.

Now, you might not believe this. I didn't at first, but it's true. Leo went back to the graveyard, had Nutty dug up, taken to a taxidermist, put back into costume, and installed in the town square.

People leave flowers everyday.

Noodles Weaver is in a slump. Oh-for twenty-two and depressed. He's too drained to eat, too tense to sleep, blames his lapse in performance on the opposing pitchers who are out to sink his career. What's the use—he's quitting baseball!

Warren Weaver made sure the whole clubhouse heard him chew out his son. "You want to quit?" he hollered. "Be a failure? A flop? I thought I raised a man, not a coward!"

Noodles was intent. "I know you care about me, dad, and I've always appreciated it, but for once in my life I'd like to think for myself."

Warren lashed out—"I knew it! I always knew it. You'll never amount to anything!"

Noodles turned and walked away.

I approached Warren. "You want I should talk to him?"

"It won't do any good," he said. "He's blowing his whole future!"

Figuring a few encouraging words might lighten his load, I joined Noodles at his locker, pointed to the untouched plate of spaghetti beside him. "You didn't eat your pasta."

"Not hungry," he mumbled.

"Well, that's a fine how-dee-do," I remarked. "Doc goes to the trouble of making her *Pasta la Squeamish* and this is how you thank her?"

He held it out to me. "Here, you take it." I took it. I love Doc's *Pasta la Squeamish*.

"I hear you're quitting," I said with a mouthful.

"That's right. You heard my dad. I'm a failure, a flop, I'll never amount to anything. Truth is I don't even know if baseball is what I want, that's dad's department. I never thought about going pro, that's dad's department. He pushed me into baseball the day I was born. All my diapers had the number nine."

"Relax, kid," I soothed, "you're going through a rough patch, but you're just overdue. Some of the game's biggest stars had slumps. But they were resilient, tenacious, never lost sight of their goal…"

"Oh, cut it out, McKay!" Noodles snapped. "You're just saying what everyone else says and it's all bullcrap!"

"Look, I can see you're angry at yourself, and at the world, and I know how that feels. In school, I struck out more than usual, and I'd get grumpy and moody and lash out…But then I saw the effect I was having. Not only was I hurting myself, I was hurting those around me. I was contagious. My teammates were catching my slump. I had to stop acting like a victim and approach life in a more positive way…As a result, I am the exceedingly well-adjusted man you see before you today."

I mugged a goofy grin. Noodles laughed and said, "I'm sorry, Mister McKay. I'd never wanna hurt my teammates. I'm such a sap sometimes."

"That's true," I agreed, "but you're a sap with a Major League future."

Noodles' lips curled to a smile. "You really think so?"

"You're a natural. Like Roy Hobbs."

"Who's Roy Hobbs?"

"The Natural."

"Natural what?"

"It's a movie. A classic. Watch it. You'll thank me."

Noodles eyes twinkled. "You really believe I could go all the way to the bigs?"

"I never lie, I'm well-adjusted. Now go un-sap yourself."

CHAPTER THIRTY SIX

Noodles swung at the first pitch—his bat *exploded*! A spear of splintered wood *rocketed* into the stands, barely missing the sleeping yokel in the front row!

I retrieved the splintered spear, inspected the bat and saw clear evidence of tampering. A hole had been drilled into the thick end and sawdust was packed into the hole. In baseball this is known as a "corked bat." In life it is known as "cheating."

I ushered Noodles into the clubhouse, handed him the corked bat. "Did your father put you up to this?"

He lowered his head in guilt. "No."

"So you did this on your own?"

"I just wanted a quicker swing."

"You could have killed that yokel in the front row."

"I'd never mean to kill anybody."

"I'm not so sure I believe you," I scolded. "You're old enough to know right from wrong and you chose wrong."

"I was desperate."

"So you cheated."

"Lotsa guys cheat."

"That's your defense? Lotsa guys cheat? Listen, my boy, this is an important time in your life. You're becoming a man. What kind of man do you want to be? You have two choices. Honest or scumbag."

"Honest," Noodles was quick to answer.

"I don't think so," I challenged. "Honesty used to be the best policy, but it doesn't seem to be trending at the moment. You proved it when you cheated. And cheating is just another way of lying. And lying only works if people believe you and who's going to believe a liar like you?"

"I am not a liar."

"Yes, you are. You have no character. Forget baseball and go into politics."

Noodles shuddered at the thought. "I'm sorry," he whimpered. "I thought it would help me and I was wrong. Please don't tell anybody."

"I'll keep this between us as long as you do something for me."

"Anything!"

"You know those opposing pitchers who are out to sink your promising career? Take it out on them."

CHAPTER THIRTY SEVEN

Billie Bedwedder sat at a card table next to the dugout, all set for her pre-game broadcast. She noticed Leo Merkin sneaking by—pulled him in front of her microphone for an interview.

Leo declined, saying, "Oh, no, I can't, I'm mysterious."

"Hello out there sports fans," Billie crisply announced, "we have with us today the exciting new owner of our *Clowntown Clowns*, Mister Leo Merkin. So, Leo, tell our viewers at home how you have managed to take this team up the slippery slope to the garden path of victory?"

Leo was silent.

"Say something," Billie whispered.

"What should I say?" Leo whispered back.

"Whatever comes into your head."

Leo crinkled with an idea…"Well, uh, it, uh, just might interest all of your viewers in radioland to know that Nutty Nuckleball was murdered, and one of our *Clowns* might've done it. Maybe more than one. And I'm thinking, right off the top of my head, that maybe we could take a poll. Or have a Nutty lookalike contest. Or re-create the murder right here on the field…"

I yanked Leo's dysfunctional mouth away from the microphone. "What the hell are you doing?" I demanded to know. "You promised to keep this under wraps."

"Springer, old buddy," he said, "you should be proud of me. I saw an opportunity and seized it. This'll be great publicity. The public loves a good murder."

It was time for damage control, so I took Leo's place in front of the microphone and made things worse.

"Oh, look who's joined us," Billie proclaimed. "The *Clowns* general manager, Springer McKay."

"Yes, I am," I acknowledged. "And I think it's important to point out that there is no actual proof that anyone connected with the *Clowntown Clowns* committed murder. A gang could've come up from Chicago. Al Capone used to have a place up here in the woods. He could have relatives nearby…"

Like I said, made things worse.

Word got back to Ernie Wacker. He's not sending a scout. "Not to a team with a cloud of murder hanging over it," he said. "What kind of an outfit are you running up there?"

"A winning outfit!" was my snap answer, until I thought to add, "Ernie, my good man, your worries are over, the murderer has been apprehended and was in no way a member of our *Clown* organization."

"*Prove* it!"

CHAPTER THIRTY EIGHT

The next morning team captain Duke Rudolf summoned me to a players' meeting at the Animal Bar. We gathered in the Domination Room, not in use at the moment.

Cricket Monsoon stood in back, poised to take notes.

Rabbi Melman was ill-at-ease being in this "Den of sin."

Scraps told him not to worry. "The sin doesn't start till happy hour."

Duke called the meeting to order. "So what do you say, guys, we're in second place behind the *Kickashit Noballers*, is it too much to ask for a living wage?"

"Yeah," Iggy confessed, "if I had more money I could afford to get laid. It ain't easy being deprived."

Duke soldiered on. "Look, guys, we're at the top of our game. We beat every team we meet."

"They're afraid if they win we'll kill 'em," snickered Scraps.

"Okay, enough with the clever wordplay," Duke went on. "I love the game, you love the game, the game should love us back. We are the future of baseball and we're being exploited."

"What's exploited?" asked Cookie.

Scraps explained. "It's when you hafta pay taxes unless you're rich."

"Or when you come to realize our weekly pay is less than a ticket to a major league game," Duke pointed out.

Streamline rose up and said, "Gentlemen, I agree with Duke. We're winners. We deserve to be treated with dignity. And there's no dignity in crappy food and crummy motels. We should at least get a per diem."

"What's a per diem?" asked Cookie.

Allstate rattled off in Spanish. Duke translated. "He says 'It's a daily allowance for living expenses'."

"How did he know that?"

"He speaks Latin."

"I just thought of something awful," said Cookie. "A strike could cancel our season with no money at all."

"That's right," said Stubby, "the 1972 Major League strike canceled 86 games, and the 1981 strike canceled 713 games, but nothing beats the 1994-95 strike which canceled the postseason and the World Series."

"Any other fascinatin' facts, Mister know-it-all?" sniped Scraps.

"Sure," said Stubby, "Babe Ruth wore a cabbage leaf under his cap to keep cool."

Ron Rigler spoke up. "Sorry, boys, but I cannot support this insane idea. Dad despised unions. When his employees went on strike, we had to let the gardener go and our plants died."

Duke chose to ignore that and pointed at me. "McKay here is a union guy. He's on our side, isn't that right, McKay?"

I knew this was coming. My turn at bat, so I said, "I like what I'm seeing here. You're thinking for yourselves, expressing your opinions. I've been on strike with the Writers Guild, so I know where you're coming from…But is this the right time? You guys are on a roll. Would it be smart to stop playing…?"

Virgil interrupted. "I thought you were on our side, McKay."

"I am, but…"

"Did the strike get what you wanted?" he asked.

"A little more money…"

"Do you hear that, boys?" Duke interjected. "They got a raise!"

Leo entered, spotted the boys and said, "Whoops, wrong room."

He turned to leave. Duke blocked his way. "Mister Merkin, you're just the man we want to see."

Leo was trapped. "I gotta pee…"

"Hold it in," Duke said with determination. "The boys and I have been talking and we are demanding that you raise our pay."

"Oh, no," Leo mumbled, "I…I can't…"

Rabbi Melman spoke up. "Colleagues, we have our answer, I move we take a vote. All those in favor of going on strike…"

Leo caved. "Okay, okay, I'll raise your pay."

Rabbi thanked the Lord. The boys trotted off in victory!

I complimented Leo on his generosity.

He said he'd do anything to save the great game of baseball.

CHAPTER THIRTY NINE

Cricket Monsoon called, inviting me to the Animal Bar to witness "democracy in action."

I found the girls in the Domination Room, not in use at the moment. They were huddled around Luscious O'Boy who was wracked with tears.

"Is she okay?" I asked Cricket.

"Luscious is crestfallen," she explained. "Heinie pulled out early and she's taking it hard."

"The dumb shit promised to marry me!" wailed Luscious. "Then, before that diamond lights my finger, he calls it off! He's nothin' but a heartbreakin' dumbass, but I'll get even. Daddy and my brothers'll settle the score. I support them, they support me."

Cricket pounded her stiletto heel on a table. "Okay, ladies, I've called us together today to talk about the movies we make for Mayor Clown."

Warbles of recognition.

"Now, the Mayor is an honorable man," Cricket continued. "At least that's what he keeps telling us. But who can believe a man who charges us for lingerie and condoms and spermicidal wipes. We should be paid a daily per diem for business expenses!"

Bursts of agreement.

Cricket pressed on. "Now, as we all know, it's not easy being a sexual superwoman. We work diligently to make our scenes look real. And, as functioning members of the motion picture industry, we deserve residuals—royalties—a piece of the pie!"

Cheers and applause!

"Ya sure," affirmed Brunhilda, "no more two-for-vun sale."

"You betcha," Brunhelga agreed, "full price for treesomes."

"I'd settle for star billing," warbled Cloris, the bow-legged contortionist.

"If I made more money I could stop livin' at home," said Destiny. "I don't like the way Pa looks at me…Ma, too."

After a moment of commiseration Cricket forged ahead. "So here's what we'll do. We'll meet with the Mayor, explain our position, and we'll get what *we* deserve or he'll get what *he* deserves."

"I know what I deserve," sniffed Luscious. "I deserve to see Heinie Pratt naked on his hands and knees, cleaning my toilet with a toothbrush in his teeth."

A chorus of *"Way to go, girl!"*

"So what do you think, Mister McKay?" Cricket asked.

Once again my turn at bat. "Well," I said, "the toothbrush idea is novel, your demands are unique, yet reasonable, you have every right to be taken seriously."

I was hugged by a gaggle of girls.

CHAPTER FORTY

Deep in a dream where I'm trapped in an elevator with Uma Thurman, there was a *POUNDING* at my door!

I unwrapped myself from Uma's clinging embrace and answered to a musket pointed at my nose, said musket being held by a mountainous man with a moth-eaten beard that stunk of skunk. Lurking behind him was a trio of sour young men eager to turn me to jello.

The man introduced himself as Luscious O'Boy's daddy, Lucius O'Boy, who rumbled, "Me'n my sons came to talk about that cock-knocker Heinie Pratt."

"Could we reschedule this meeting?" I suggested. "I don't think clearly in bikini briefs."

Daddy pushed his face into mine and growled, "People around here look down on us folks 'cause we're from the other side of the tracks. But there ain't no tracks no more, 'cause there ain't no train no more. And there ain't gonna be no more Pratt 'cause he tells my darlin' daughter he's rich, then leaves her high and dry, that fucker's gonna die!"

I tried reason. "Take it easy, Mister O'Boy, I'm sure this can all be worked out."

"Okay," he ordered, "*you* talk that peckerhead into marriage or *yer* gonna die!"

The *Clowns* keep on winning and Heinie is not the reason why. His behavior is increasingly erratic. He forgets. Is delusional. Calls me Steve Garvey.

Today he thought we were playing the *New York Giants* and put himself in to pinch hit in the ninth with the bases loaded. We tried to take him off the field, he soaked us with the garden hose, causing us to forfeit, terminating our winning streak.

My players and coaches were infuriated. Just when things were going right Pratt screws it. The man is ruining their futures. Something's gotta be done.

Spook Spindler nudged me, his long face infused with an idea. "My cousin, Rummy, knows a guy whose sister is a hit man. Want me to give him a call?"

Heinie wasn't in his room, or in the Big Rack Lounge, which got me to worrying. The poor man could be floundering in a fog.

Wolfgang tooled me past a pawnshop, a tattoo parlor, a fireworks tent, and up to Heinie on a bench in the town square. He was talking to the stuffed Nutty statue. I stood by and observed.

"Nope," he told Nutty, "Bob Feller didn't start today, it was Bob Gibson. Never get your Bobs mixed up, animals of a whole different persuasion."

He paused to listen to what the stuffed Nutty was saying, then replied, "Well, it's nice'a you to ask, my season's goin' great, keepin' my average at three-twenty, thirty homers, a hundred some RBIs, not bad for a veteran."

Heinie noticed me standing nearby. "Hey, Garvey, how they hangin'? I'm doin' a post-game interview. Gotta be kind to the press even if they do eat shit."

I crossed over to him and said, "Heinie, you're talking to a dead man."

"Oh, him'n me were teammates with the *Pirates*." He turned to Tinky and said, "You were a real stinkpot, Tink. A guy like you was meant to die."

"It's late, Heinie," I urged. "Way past your curfew."

Heinie lowered his head, his hands began to shake as he muttered... "I'm bein' followed by strange men."

"What do they look like?"

"Creatures from a lagoon."

"The O'Boys," I noted. "They want you to reconsider your marriage to Luscious."

"Nope," Heinie stated, "can't do, no can do. That girl never stops yammerin', always screechin' along to that rappity-yaketty crap on her phone while I'm tryin' to show her my lusty side, takes all the romance out of it, makes my dangler droop and, believe you me, I could teach sex in high school..."

I jumped in—"Heinie, you hurt Luscious."

"I can't help if she finds me irresistible?"

"Go talk to her," I said. "Be honest. Tell her you're not rich."

"I ain't talkin' to her," he volleyed, "you talk to her, your tongue is more silver than mine."

"Alright, alright, I'll talk to her. But on one condition. You have a nice long talk with Doc Squeamish, okay?"

Heinie gave a weak "uh-huh," gazed at me through cloudy eyes and moaned, "Somethin' ain't right, Garvey. Get the wobblies...Cloggin' in the noggin...I can't remember where I live..."

CHAPTER FORTY ONE

I told Doc Squeamish about Heinie's condition…"At first I wasn't sure if he was failing or just plain bonkers."

"A bit of both," she diagnosed. "There's no doubt he's always been an oddball, but lately I've noticed he forgets, wanders around in a state of confusion. Before every game he comes up to me and says, 'I lost my glove'. 'Where did you put my glove?' 'I can't play without my glove'."

Doc paused, then said, "My husband had dementia. A slow, vacant death. Heinie needs me."

Wolfgang motored me to the Animal Bar where I intended to straighten-out Heinie's wayward love life.

Luscious O'Boy was at the bar downing jello shots. A black veil covered her face and not her breasts.

I spoke to the veil. "Could I see you for a minute?"

She peeked out. "Okay, but no rough stuff, I'm in mourning."

"Who died?" I asked.

"Romance," she sighed.

"Luscious, I don't mean to poke my nose in your business, but this thing with Heinie, it may not be the perfect match."

"I know," she said. "He always wants my side of the bed."

"See, it'll never work," I said. "So take my advice and forget all about Heinie Pratt."

"I'm not good enough, is that what you think?"

"No, that's not what I think…Have you considered the age difference?"

"Girls marry old guys 'cause young guys are babies."

"Luscious," I pleaded, "listen very closely. *Heinie Pratt is not rich!*"

She paused to absorb this…"You think I can do better?"

I hit her with my sincerest smile and said, "I do."

"I accept!!" she squealed, and ran off shouting—"Hey, everybody, Mister McKay and me are *engaged!*"

I stood there…in traction.

Tempest Bedwedder poked me alive, saying, "That went well."

"I've had better days," I said, noticing her arm in a sling. "What happened to you?"

"Klutzy me. Slipped in the shower."

"Yeah, sure…You should be more careful."

"I can't help the way I feel, Springer. I love you and Royal will just have to get used to it. I'm not his property, I'm emancipated."

Ralph Dalton Futz called, stuck in traffic on the 405, late for his Zumba class. "Springer, dear fellow," he said, "in our quest to rid the world of clown slayers I have uncovered a significant and compelling clue…It seems that some twenty years ago Tinky Farzock was married and apparently had a son. The identity of the alleged son is unknown… Or is it?"

CHAPTER FORTY TWO

Our winning ways have renewed interest in our team. Ticket sales are up. The fans are back in the stands. Mayor Clown hosted a dance in our honor so he could take all the credit.

The walls of the Bed & Barn barn clattered to the rhythms of Pete Clowndowski & his Polka Potentates.

My boys were seated at an autograph table, a cluster of flirtatious local girls gathered around them. A swarm of local boys watched with bloodshed in their eyes.

At the bar, I ordered a seven buck beer from a grandmotherly bartender wearing a coonskin cap. Large letters on her tee-shirt proclaimed—*I Slept With Dean Martin.*

I spotted Royal Bedwedder at the end of the bar, acknowledged him with a neighborly wave. He fired a beer bottle past my head.

"Ball four!" I boldly announced.

Royal lurched up to me, hissing—"You ain't never fuckin' nobody's wife again."

His bumpkin buddies "Ooooooooed!"

Having scored the deciding blow, Royal puffed out his chest and sauntered off in victory.

A huge pair of hands jerked me around and I was face-to-beard with Daddy O'Boy, his breath reminiscent of expired liverwurst. "Now that you perposed to my Luscious you ain't gonna break her heart like that other bunghole, are ya?"

"Look," I said, "let me explain…"

He cut me short—"Yer rich, ain't ya?"

"Not really," I said. "All my money's tied-up in debts."

My attempt at wit slid through his ears.

"You married?" Daddy demanded to know.

"Not that I know of."

"I'm breakin' in wife number five," he proudly stated. "If I'd'a been one'a them Mormons I could'a had 'em all at once." He gave my back a whack. "Welcome to the family."

I had to put a stop to this right now. "Listen, Daddy, I think there's been a misunderstanding…"

I was interrupted by a sudden commotion! A crowd circled around to watch Mayor Clown and Sheriff Clowndale in a shoving match.

"Let's settle this election right now," challenged the Mayor.

"Fine by me," the Sheriff agreed. He raised his fists, ready for combat. "Put 'em up!"

The Mayor stomped on the Sheriff's toe. "OW!"

The Sheriff stomped the Mayor's toe. "OW!"

A flurry of toe-stomping, "OW! OW! OW! OW!" followed by both men whipping out their pistols and, silly me, I stepped between them, shouting—"Stop before someone gets killed!'

"What's wrong with that," Royal's voice lurked from behind.

I turned with a neighborly wave.

Royal sucker-punched me!

His bumpkin buddies "Oooooooooed!"

I felt my jaw. Still there. The local boys began to crowd around my players. I turned to face Royal, my lips curled in a bloody smile. "I could punch you back," I calmly told him, "but it could start a fight and you could lose a tooth. Me and my boys aren't looking for trouble. We came in peace, we intend to leave in peace."

Giving a John Wayneish hunch to my shoulders, I led my troops to the barn door.

"Hey, McKay!" Royal shouted. "Ever been challenged to a duel?"

I stopped, turned to him. "Uh…no, not really."

Royal swaggered up to me and said—"Noon tomorrow, town square, be there!"

"Oooooooo!"

So there I was, back-to-back with Royal Bedwedder, holding up a pistol rented from Mayor Clown.

An audience of yokels munched popcorn as the Mayor laid out the rules. "Ten paces—turn—fire—may the luckiest man win." He began to count. "*One, two...*"

Daddy O'Boy and his sour sons, swooped in from the crowd—"You people keep yer paws off'a McKay," Daddy yelled, "he's gonna make a virgin of my darlin' Luscious."

Royal turned to Daddy and snickered, "That'd take a miracle."

Daddy and his sons lunged at Royal and his buddies. Fists were flung! Crotches were kicked! Screams were heard!

"Order!" the Mayor shouted. "We must have order!! These citizens paid good money to see this show, let's get on with it."

I was back to being back-to-back.

The Mayor counted, "One...two..."

The *Clowntown Clowns* burst through the crowd brandishing baseball bats. They grunted in frenzied harmony as they swung wildly at the frightened crowd!

Max Doody held a bat over the Mayor's head and growled, "Feel like sayin' *three?*"

My death was put on hold.

The yokels demanded their money back.

CHAPTER FORTY THREE

I was leaving the ballpark after today's game when I noticed a lone figure standing at the plate. He swung his bat at an imaginary ball, watched it launch, rounded the bases in victory.

I greeted Bob Snooks as he crossed the plate.

"Nice cut," I said.

"I was scouted by the *Chicago White Sox* in high school," he said, "but dad made me join the business. I hated bein' a dentist, all them mucky mouths. I'm a born ballplayer. All I want is a chance."

I put a comforting hand on Snooks' shoulder, "We'll see, Bob. Check with me later."

Snooks pointed up. "That ball just landed on Mars."

Ever since Noodles told Warren to back off he's been giving his son the silent treatment. That is, until a mysterious man arrived on the scene.

Short and swarthy, decked out in a Panama hat, slick suit, shoes fresh off the alligator, Cisco Torcido watched the team workout. He took notes, chatted with the players, word quickly spread that he was a scout. The players gathered around like he was the King of Siam.

Later, in the clubhouse, Warren Weaver was forbidding his son to have any dealings with Torcido. "I've seen his type before," he warned, "he's a swindler, preys on young prospects. He'll take over your life and steal you blind."

"But he says he's a big sports agent," said Noodles.

"He's a phony."

"You don't know that."

"I'll tell you what I do know," said Warren as he walked out. "Torcido means *'crooked'* in Spanish?"

Spook Spindler overheard, told me Cisco Torcido is the real deal. "He's one'a them superagents. Wants everybody to kiss his ass."

The *Clowntown Clowns* played brilliant defense, spectacular offense. Virgil Weathers only gave up three hits in eight innings. Ron Rigler swiftly mopped up the ninth. We routed the *Beaverbrook Bullheads* by a score of 9-zip.

I Googled a Spanish dictionary. Torcido does mean crooked in Spanish. Had to check this guy out.

Spotted him having a beer in the Big Rack Lounge, introed myself. He handed me his card—*Cisco Torcido. Chairman and CEO. Goldbrick Sports Enterprises. New York City.*

I don't represent any particular team," he told me. "I'm what you call a roving scout. My corporation is always looking to develop new properties."

"Sort of like slave traders?"

"Is that supposed to be funny?"

"Not for the slaves."

"Look, smartass, I am a legitimate trader. I turn jocks into millionaires, and there's someone on your roster who might fit the bill."

The next day, Cisco Torcido was ready to sign Noodles Weaver to a personal management contract.

Ink hadn't hit paper when Warren Weaver rushed up. "Oh, here you are, son," he said, "I've been looking all over for you because I, well, I want to apologize for being such a jerk. You're a grown boy, you should think for yourself, so if you want to quit baseball I won't stand in your way."

"Thanks, dad," smiled Noodles, "but there's a change in plans."

Warren looked bewildered. "Change?... What are you talking about?"

"Mister Torcido wants to sign me," Noodles grinned. "He told me it won't be long before I'm in the majors. I have greatness in me."

Warren turned on Torcido. "I am not gonna stand by and watch my boy get robbed by a shyster like you."

Torcido rankled me a glance. "Look, McKay, I don't need this shit."

Noodles pushed his father away, shouting—*"Get out of my life!"*

CHAPTER FORTY FOUR

In today's loss to the *Dead Lake Loons* we had the tying run on third, two outs in the ninth, when Heinie darted out of the dugout, put himself in as a pinch runner and got picked off. When he was heckled by the *Dead Lake* dugout he sprayed the *Loons* with the garden hose leading to the customary bench-clearing brawl.

Only minor scrapes and bruises. We were lucky this time, but there can't be a next time. Heinie has a problem. His problem is my problem. It's time to tell him it's over.

It was easier than I thought.

Heinie took a seat next to me in the clubhouse and said, "Well, Garvey, I been thinkin' It's high time I stepped down as skipper, ain't no fun no more. Doody can manage the team, so apologize to the boys for me, tell 'em I forgive 'em for makin' fun'a me, if I were me I'd make fun'a me, too."

He fell silent.

"Gee, Heinie, I don't know what to say," I said, "I'd sure hate to see the *Clown* organization lose a man with your skill and expertise. How about you stick around, be our special consultant?"

"Well, that suits me just fine," Heinie grinned. "I been thinkin' about settlin' in Clowntown. Got my eye on that Squeamish gal. She's a pretty hot toddy for her advanced age."

A rapping at my door. "Who is it!"

"It's me, Peewee," a whispery voice answered.

I scrambled out of bed, opened the door. "Peewee, what are you doing here? It's four in the morning."

"I'm an early riser," he said with twitchy desperation in his eyes. "Can I come in? It's awful important."

Peewee entered, handed me a slingshot and a small bag of peas. "Mister McKay, I want you to have these," he said, "they're evidence. Y'see, I don't use a pea shooter like the other guys. I use a slingshot. And I was afraid Sheriff Clowndale might take my slingshot and peas, so I hid them in that old garage so nobody would find 'em."

Peewee couldn't hold back the tears. "It's no use, Mister McKay, I gotta confess…"

He squeezed his eyes shut and boldly announced—"I killed Nutty Nuckleball."

"Uh-huh," I said. "And is there any reason why you would do that?"

"It had to be me," Peewee moaned "I'm a sureshot with a slingshot. I aimed for Nutty's neck and hit a bullseye. I never thought it would kill him. I meant to use a regular pea, I guess I shot a pointy one."

"You knew about the pointy peas?"

"Yeah, I carve them myself and use them for hunting, They're great for killing rabbits and squirrels. I'm an assassin. Lock me up."

Sensing a sure-fire appearance on *60 Minutes*, Sheriff Clowndale locked the boy up.

The Clam Falls Crime Lab found traces of curare' on the prickly-pointed peas. But where in the Wisconsin woods did the curare' come from?... Then I realized there are several sites online that offer deals on poisons. Thanks to technology, murder is easier to commit than ever.

I'm about to call Futz. Futz calls me. The guy is psychic. I swear.

"Springer, old bean," he said, "tell me your keen eye for behavior, unerring knack for deduction and proclivity for sticking your nose where it does not belong, has led you to our murderer."

He was right about my nose, but I wasn't ready to tell him I had a confession from a nine-year-old boy.

"I found the murder weapon," I told him. "A prickly-pointed pea."

"Ha!" he chortled…"Seriously, what is the weapon?"

"A prickly-pointed pea," I affirmed. "Points sharp enough to puncture the skin."

"A prickly-pointed pea!" bubbled Futz. "How wonderfully bizarre! Reminiscent of scrimshaw, the practice of carving on the tusks of walruses and teeth of the sperm whale. I'll use prickly-pointed peas in my next screenplay."

I headed over to the Sheriff's office. Daddy O'Boy and his sour sons were two steps behind me. I whipped around and said, "Don't look now, but I think I'm being followed."

Daddy smiled through teeth of rotted corn. "Just keepin' an eye out fer ya, son. Makin' sure yew'll show up for the weddin' come Saturday!"

"I'll check my calendar to see if I'm free."

Daddy and sons didn't get the joke. They are one.

I took refuge in the Sheriff Clowndale's office. Judge Percy Clownlaw was bailing out his son. He knows Peewee is no murderer, the boy only thinks he is.

"I think your son is being set-up," I told the Judge, "but I have to make sure."

"Peewee," I asked, "where did you get the curare'?"

He shot me an absent look…"What's a curare'?"

Judge Clownlaw pronounced sentence and confiscated his son's phone for a day.

CHAPTER FORTY FIVE

Cisco Torcido signed Ron Rigler to a personal management contract. Those who didn't get chosen were disheartened, disillusioned, why do rats inherit the earth?

Rigler lorded over his teammates. "Yes, it's true," he swaggered. "Thanks to my good friend and mentor, Cisco Torcido, I am about to enter the hallowed halls of Major League baseball. I always knew I'd be the chosen one. The first to break out of this bleak reality. I am now a professional, not amateurs like you..." He jerked a look at Virgil Weathers. "...Or a has-been who doesn't know the game is over."

Virgil bolted up—swung at Rigler and missed!

Rigler snatched Virgil's baseball card off his locker door, ripped it in half, not a good move. A player's card is sacred. Rigler had committed a baseball sin.

The entire team piled on him, punching away while he screamed—*"My fingers! Don't break my fingers!"*

I inserted myself into the skirmish and scuffled things to order without injury if you don't count my emerging black eye.

Rigler rose to his feet, snatched up his gear and walked out saying, "Come see me play sometime."

The players muttered their way to batting practice. Virgil sat, staring at his ripped baseball card. Figuring he might need a sympathetic ear, I lent him mine. "Feel like talking?"

"I'd like to kill that jackass," Virgil griped. "He'll never make it to the bigs like I did."

He joined the halves of his card together, carefully taped it back on his locker. "This here card is my prize," he told me. "my dream come true… Least it was until my arm got sore. I figured I'd play through it, it'd take care of itself. Turned out I tore a tendon in my elbow, ended with a crooked arm and out'a pro ball…till now."

Virgil held up a baseball, gripped it with his knuckles. "This here 'knuckler' is my ticket back to the bigs. Hitters can't hit it. Umpires can't see it. Now, if y'all will excuse me, I gotta go whip the competition."

Spook Spindler appeared with a nudge. "Better believe what Virgil tells you." he said. "He's better than he ever was. The scouts are gonna notice him. Also the pitching coach who got him there."

Spook reached in his back pocket, whipped out a plastic bottle. "Perhaps I can interest you in a bottle of Rightway's latest product—*Holy HairGrow!* Guaranteed to kick those expired follicles back to life. It's no secret that silver mane of yours is gettin' thin in back."

I bought six bottles.

I had to come to terms with the loss of Ron Rigler. The kid's a suspect. Did I let a murderer walk out the door?... Nah, Rigler wouldn't have the nerve. Bullies are colossal cowards.

CHAPTER FORTY SIX

A note for me at the front desk. Spike Clownhowser read it and does not approve of non-married couples capitulating, it stains the sheets.

The note read: *Room 12. A gallon of Moose Tracks. You-Know-Who.*

I hesitated at Tempest's door. It was time to lay it on the line. I had to tell her there's no future in loving a dead man.

The door swung open. Tempest stood there, strikingly seductive in a camouflage nightie and slippers with antlers. She pulled me into the room and lipped me a scorcher. Once recovered, I saw she was sporting a black eye.

"What's with the shiner?" I asked.

"Ran into a door," she replied, pointing to my eye. "What's your story?"

"Ran into a fist."

"Poor baby," she purred, pulling in for another kiss.

I eased her away. "He did this to you, didn't he?"

"I don't know..." she shrugged. "Maybe I deserved it. I told Royal I was gonna leave and we had a fight and he blames you. I told him it was my decision, but he never listens to what I say, doesn't see me as an actual person. I'm his hotsy totsy, his yummy mummy, his booty box. Sex with him is like a vaccination."

She threw herself on the bed. "Aw, what can I say?" she sobbed. "I'm dumb, ignorant, nobody ever taught me how to choose a life partner, it's ad-lib from the first kiss…But now, when I see you, I feel this tingle of arousal. I yearn to express my true sexual self before my libido takes a hike. So, how about you gather me in your arms and make mad, passionate love to me."

It would've been rude to refuse.

CHAPTER FORTY SEVEN

The players are winning and feeling unappreciated. Duke cornered Leo and told him if he doesn't keep his promise to raise their pay they're going on strike!

Leo immediately promised not only to raise their pay, but to *double* it!

The players hoot and hollered onto the field!

I threw a brotherly arm around Leo. "I'm proud of you, my friend, that was a kind and generous act."

"No it wasn't," he said.

"Why not?"

"Remember Skeets Jaggler?"

"Your celebrity business manager."

"Fled to Mexico."

Today is payday with no pay to pay so, in desperation, I decided to keep the team afloat by using a small sum I'd stashed away to keep me breathing during bouts of unemployment. I call it my emergency fund, now it's my loaves and fishes. Let's see how far I can stretch it.

Not far. After only a few days my account was down to half a loaf and no fishes and I had visions of being sent to a debtor's prison where I'd be tied up and forced to listen to Pat Boone records.

I decided to ease my monetary anxiety at the Big Rack Lounge. Spike Clownhowser's drink of the day was the "Tahitian Twizzler," an exotic blend of strawberry rum, lime rum, mango rum, rhubarb rum, bubble gum rum...I ordered a Pabst.

Mayor Clown slithered onto the stool next to me, saying, "McKay, I'll get right to the point. You and your mysterious partner have left me no choice but to seize your property in the name of *eminent domain!*"

He slapped a legal document on the bar. Translated from lawyerese it stated that the local government, represented by Mayor Mongrel J. Clown, had the right to seize the ballpark and its land for public use.

I knew all about eminent domain. Researched it for a script about young real estate hustlers called *The Escrow Kids*.

Armed with this knowledge I fixed the Mayor with a confident gaze and said, "Y'know, hijacking private property is a serious abuse of power."

"Not hardly," Mayor Clown smugly stated. "It happens to be the Fourteenth Amendment of the U.S. Constitution." He whipped out his little Constitution book to show me.

"Why, indeed it is," I affirmed. "And did you know the Amendment also contains a Due Process Clause stating that private landowners are guaranteed a legal judgment before their land is plucked away? And that the landowner should receive just compensation which could lead to millions?... So, I'll get a lawyer, you'll get a lawyer, and we'll play Constitutional tag for the next twenty years."

The Mayor's leer wrenched to a smirk as he said, "You thought I was serous, didn't you? It was a joke, I was testing you. I'm very good at testing and I can see the kind of fella you are. You remind me of me. We're no fools. We're men of the world. When opportunity knocks we answer the bell. So, what's say you and me join forces in a little business venture?"

"I don't want to own a Flea Market."

"Neither do I," he chuckled. "Why bother with small potatoes when we can replace the ballpark with—*The Clowntown Bunny Ranch!*"

"You're gonna raise rabbits?"

"No, no," he dismissed. "I'm talking about a huge and improved Animal Bar! A sexual supermarket! A palace of porn! Fifty girls! No waiting! There's a gold mine in pussy. It's the gift that never stops giving."

132

"I liked the Flea Market better."

"Oh, come on," the Mayor pleaded, "you're passing up a golden opportunity. Alcohol used to be illegal, but there was money to be made, Congress acted, it's the national pastime. And, now, with even more money to be made, prostitution will soon be the law of the land... I even thought up a slogan—*Get a bang for your buck with a bunny!* Pretty good, huh? I have an excellent mind for slogans. So what do you think? Are you in?"

"Nah, pimping's not on my bucket list."

The Mayor morphed to darkness, slid off his stool, and said, "You'll come around McKay. Mongrel J. Clown *always* gets what he wants."

I had a sinking feeling the Mayor was right. In that script I wrote for *The Escrow Kids*, eminent domain came out on top.

CHAPTER FORTY EIGHT

I relayed the Mayor's message to Leo who swiftly packed his satchel. "That's it, we're gonna get skunked!"

"Leo, we can beat this eminent domain thing."

"It's no use," he moaned. "Big brother has raised his evil head."

He grabbed his satchel, headed for the door.

I blocked his way. "You can't just walk out on your team."

"They'll never know I'm gone."

I snatched his satchel, emptied it on the bed. "Leo, old chum, it's time for us to fight back."

We consulted a lawyer. A spry old geezer in a doo-rag and Harley leather named Clyde Burning Bush. After signing a promise to pay him with a twelve-pack of Leinenkugel he explained to us that —

"Eminent domain has never gone over with the general public, even though it's supposed to protect the general public. And any government entity, even our unscrupulous Mayor, may be within his rights to swipe the ballpark away from you. Having succeeded, he would then think he owns the ballpark even though he does not own the ballpark, because *you* do not own the ballpark. You do not own the ballpark because the land beneath the ballpark, and the rights to whatever is built on the land beneath the ballpark, belongs to the Minneheehaw Tribe of which I am the legal counsel, meaning you guys got the shaft."

In no time at all, Leo and I found ourselves at the First Clown Security Integrity Fidelity Bank & Trust Company with aces up our sleeves.

"Mayor Clown," I began, "you don't have to go through this government take-over crap. We know when we're licked. We're ready to sell you the ballpark."

The Mayor broke into an oily grin. "Oh, I love the smell of defeat. Name your price."

"As much as you can spare," Leo begged.

"We only want what we paid for it," I quickly added. "In cash."

I could hear the miserly wheels turn in the Mayor's head. "Agreed!" he said, whipping out a document and slamming it on the desk.

We signed. The Mayor paid. We wished the sucker luck.

My phone rang. Futz asked if I had anything new on the case.

I told him my nine-year-old bat boy thinks he's the murderer.

"That could very well be true," he said.

"You can't be serious."

"Dear fellow, there are slivers of madness in all God's children. That is why we have wars…But enough about that, I have solved the case."

"You're kidding. Who did it?"

"Well, my good man, based on what you have told me about the members of your organization, I can now clearly point to an individual who shows a distinct aptitude for murder. A man filled with pent-up emotions. A man ready to lash out at any time. I see your dear friend and partner, Leo Merkin!"

"Oh, c'mon," I laughed. "Leo wouldn't hurt a fly unless he swallowed it."

"You told me Merkin is the quiet type," Futz asserted, "likes to keep to himself. That's what they say about murderers."

"Well, yeah, I suppose…"

"Is Merkin impulsive?" Futz quizzed. "Does he act without thinking?"

"All the time."

"There you have it!" he rejoiced.

Futz signed off, saying, "It's been a pleasure doing business with you. Additional fees will be added to your account."

I found Futz's theory unthinkable. The whole idea is ridiculous, far-fetched. Leo Merkin a killer? Not a chance, he fainted when Snow White ate the apple. Sure, Leo's the quiet type. A private person. Never opens up about his personal life. I've known the guy for twenty years…and I don't know the guy at all.

CHAPTER FORTY NINE

Domination Room. A vote on whether or not to strike. Iggy Fanoki took a poll and the general feeling is yes and no with a few undecided.

Duke Rudolf called the meeting to order. "Okay, fellas, here's the score. Merkin promised to raise our pay, so where is it? Every time I remind him he thanks me for reminding him. Let's face it, guys he doesn't appreciate us. Doesn't respect us. We're being used and abused, it's time for us to vote."

I raised my hand. "May I say something?"

"Okay listen up, guys," said Duke, "McKay has something to say."

"Yes, I do. I want all of you to be aware that there is a good possibility you could be seen by a Major League scout."

"So where is this scout?" Iggy wanted to know. "I don't see no scout. The guy must be fictional."

A touchy situation. If I tell the boys a *Cub* scout is coming, they won't strike. But if the *Cub* scout never comes, the boys will hate me for giving them false hope.

"What I'm trying to say," I explained, "is that when a scout does show up to see you play, you might have to play."

"I thought you were with us, McKay," said Duke.

"I am. You're a winning team and deserve to be rewarded."

"You bet we do," Duke swiftly agreed. "So let's vote. All those in favor of a strike raise your hand." Hands were raised. Duke took a quick count. "It looks like it's unani...," he started to say. "Wait, Virgil didn't vote."

"Do whatever you want," Virgil muttered, "just count me out."

"Okay, one abstention," said Duke, "the vote's still unanimous. We picket the stadium tomorrow."

The boys high-fived their way out of the clubhouse.

Virgil sat alone. He showed me a letter and said…"My wife wants a divorce. Says she's tired of bein' married to a dreamer with no profession to fall back on…But I don't wanna fall back. Baseball's my profession. It's all I know how to do…Now, if ya don't mind, I'd like to feel sorry for myself."

The specter of a strike gnawed at me like a rabid hamster so, I placed another call to Ernie Wacker and was put on hold to an all-accordion band. Gave me a chance to plan my strategy.

Wacker needed proof that there are no murderers in the *Clown* organization, so I figured I'd use a stalling tactic, call it a bluff, anything to keep hope alive.

Wacker came on the line. I wound up and pitched—"The case is solved and the murderer will be brought to justice!!"

"That's great, McKay," said Wacker, "but my *Cubs* won't be scouting your *Clowns*, we decided to check out another team in your *Northwoods League*."

My heart sank to my shoes. "…What other team?"

"The *Kickapoo Hayhaulers*."

CHAPTER FIFTY

I stood helplessly by as my players and coaches picketed the entrance to the ballpark.

Billie Bedwedder, microphone in hand, boisterously called the action—"A huge howdy and hello to all you sports fans out there in sportsland! Billie Bedwedder here in front of historic Clown Memorial Stadium where our beloved *Clowntown Clowns* are staging a work stoppage! The players are slowly ambling back and forth waving picket signs that literally shriek out the words—*Unfair! We deserve respect! Clowns are people too!* An infinite congregation of local citizens have swarmed the area, hissing and booing like an embittered wind!"

Billie turned to see Leo standing next to her. "Ah, what a rare treat. I have *Clown* owner Leo Merkin here with me." She pushed the mic in his face. "Leo, give my vast audience your eagle-eye view of what is going on."

"Glad to," he said. "Today is Green Weenie Day and the Cub scouts are here."

Word raced through the picket line. "The *Cub* scouts are here!"

The boys were *electrified!*

"They sent more than one scout!"

"This is our chance."

"The biggest game of our lives!"

The team tossed away their signs and stormed into the clubhouse.

I caught up to Leo before he vanished. "Are the *Cub* scouts really here?"

"You better believe it."

"The real *Chicago Cub* scouts?"

"Right you are."

"No, I'm not.

"No, you're not," he agreed. "I invited Cub Scout Pack Four to attend. I'm their den leader and an old Tiger Cub myself. Got a merit badge for cooking. It was just a hot dog on a stick, but I dipped it in Dijon mustard and served it on a poppy seed bun…"

I grabbed Leo by the shoulders, drilled him a look. "Leo, I want you to go into that clubhouse and tell those boys the truth."

"You tell them," said Leo. "I promised my Cubs we'd run the bases."

In the clubhouse, I watched my boys laugh, horse around, ready to beat the crap out of the today's opponent, the *Scum River Cavaliers.*

I knew they'd hear the truth soon enough and I'd rather they heard it from me, so I announced—"Boys, there's something you should know. The Cub Scouts here today are a pack of children. The *Chicago Cub* scouts will not be coming."

A stunned silence, broken by Duke—"Why the hell not?"

"They decided to check out the *Hayhaulers*."

Spirits withered…Hope kicked the bucket.

"It was a stupid dream," sighed Stubby.

"Why doesn't nothin' good ever happen?" Iggy whimpered.

"Because life is shit," mumbled Scraps.

Stubby grabbed his bat and began to bang it against his locker, yelling—*"I'm almost there! Almost nowhere! Nobody knows me! Nobody cares…!"*

I snatched the bat from Stubby's grasp. "Hey, hey," I cautioned, "I don't want to hear that kind of talk from you guys. When life gives you a gut-punch shake it off and move on. I've had more than my share of disappointments. Spent years living in a cockroach-infested apartment writing things no one wanted to see. I waited tables, drove cabs, walked dogs, but I never lost sight of my goal. I never gave up, never stopped working and when opportunity knocked I was prepared to win."

My *Clowns* took the field, prepared to lose.

CHAPTER FIFTY ONE

We lost all three to *Scum Lake*, but we'll make up for it. Today, we face the *Timberville Splinters*, a team with the worst record in the league.

Game one. *Clown* blunders, boo-boos, not even close.

Game two. Rain, sleet, thunder snow as the *Splinters* were victorious. They wore galoshes.

Game three. A warm sunny day, clouded by the *Timberville* players hazing the *Clowns*, calling them *"Murderer's Row,"* wondering if they'd get the electric chair, the firing squad, or the gas chamber.

Splinters 12, *Clowns* 0.

Six straight losses.

Our team was unraveling.

My boys were accusing each other of murder.

Rabbi Melman was sitting shiva to mourn the dead.

2 a.m. Some yokel decided to use his leaf blower.

I laid in a trance, suspects cart-wheeling through my brain...

Heinie wanted to murder Tinky.

Doody wanted to strangle Tinky.

Spook wanted to kill Tinky.

These three had a lot on common. They had motives. As opposed to a sweet kid like Noodles who seems to have no motive at all. Or does he? And what about his father?

Tinky Farzock was a father. Had a son.
My boys spoke of their fathers.
Stubby's father never raised him.
Virgil's father was a bum.
Rabbi's father liked to hug.
Cookie's father never hugged.
Scraps never knew his father.
Iggy's father took a hike.
Duke's father broke his arm.
Allstate's father never spoke.
Streamline's father was his friend...
The leaf blower snorted to a *stop*!

    I blinked out of my trance and realized this was a very long list. If I was ever going to solve this case I needed to narrow it down. The one thing I knew for sure was that all of the above were in the dugout at the exact time Nutty was bumped off...Unless, of course, the perpetrator wasn't actually "in" the dugout, just "close" to the dugout.

    Mayor Clown? Royal Bedwedder? Bumpkin buddies? Daddy? Sour sons? So much for narrowing down.

    Streamline got shelled especially hard today. After the game, I found him slumped at his locker, head down, mumbling to himself..."I try too hard. Every pitch is a mistake. I'll never make it in this game."

    He paused, looked up at me, tears in his eyes..."Mister McKay, my arm. It hurts. Hurts real bad."

    Doc Squeamish's analysis was a strained shoulder. "Pitching is a very unnatural action," she explained. "Arms that throw smoke can burn out. Streamline's left arm is probably twice as old as his right, and throwing a slider or a curve may have caused a ligament sprain, or bursitis, or irritation of the ulnar nerve, commonly known as the funny bone. I'll treat his arm with ice, massage, my special salve of willow bark and a dollop of Old Grand-dad. In the meantime, the best treatment is rest, don't you agree?"

    "I'd never want to hurt his chances."

    "Oh, one more thing," Doc added. "I asked Heinie Pratt to marry me and he accepted."

CHAPTER FIFTY TWO

The Men's Club's annual spaghetti and meatball bash is tonight. The *Clowntown Clowns* have been invited.

My boys don't want to go. They're losers. They'll be riddled with bullets.

"Well, that's a fine way of looking at things," I told them. "If you don't show, you'll be branded as cowards. But you are not cowards. You are brave, you are strong, you are not afraid to face adversity."

"What's adversity?" asked Iggy.

"The kiss'a death," snapped Scraps.

The Clowntown Men's Club is located in a pre-fab aluminum Quonset Hut, circa 1942. Mayor Mongrel J. Clown stood at the entrance directing Royal and his bumpkin buddies to—"Check your guns here! The State Safety Inspector has paid us a *surprise visit.*"

They deposited their weapons and, stop me if I'm wrong, but the State Safety Inspector bore an amazing resemblance to a bearded Exotica doing her impression of Meryl Streep as a man.

I headed my boys into the room, Mayor Clown blocked our way. "What are you bums doing here?"

"We were invited."

"Well, now you're dis-invited."

"I liked it better the first time."

The Mayor's eyes narrowed. "Listen, McKay, I can have the bunch of you thrown out."

"And the bunch of us will tear this place apart," I threatened.

My boys *growled* to show how tough they were.

Mayor Clown relented with a heartless chuckle. "Okay, okay, have it your way. If you dare to mingle with your disgruntled fans, do it at your own risk."

The hors d'oeuvres table was laden with a reclining nude woman sculpted in raw venison. Men poked at her with Triscuits. Her breasts were the first to go.

I caught a glimpse of Tempest tending bar, ambled over. "Excuse me, ma'am, but I was led to believe this was a stag affair."

"I talk dirty," Tempest explained, "so the men see me as one of them…I get off at nine, bring some mint chocolate chip."

Mayor Clown called for everyone to take their seats at the horseshoe-shaped banquet table. On the other side of the horseshoe sat Royal Bedwedder and his bumpkin buddies. Royal pointed his finger at me, shot, blew away the smoke, coughed to make it look real.

The Mayor commenced the proceedings with—"Welcome, boys, lots of yummy things on tonight's menu. The Animal Girls are here with their wet titty extravaganza!"

The men howled and feigned masturbation.

Rabbi and Cookie got up and left.

"But first off," the Mayor continued, "why do blondes wear underwear?"

"To keep their ankles warm," the men droned in unison.

"What do you call a blonde with pigtails?" asked the Mayor.

"A blowjob with handlebars," chanted the men.

"And last, but not least," said the Mayor, "why are blondes so easy to get in bed?"

"*Who cares!*" the men called out.

"Right you are, boys," the Mayor went on. "And now, while Chef Clownburger serves up our spaghetti and meatballs, the Animal Girls told me they have a special treat for us. Take it away, Animal Girls!"

Blackout. The room ruffled with hormonal tremors.

Lights up! Three large cupcakes stood before the men. Their legs began to tap-dance. Heads popped out of the tops of the cupcakes.

"I'm Cricket!"

"I'm Brunhilda!"

"I'm Brunhelga!"

"We are your *desserts!*"

The men hooted like hyenas as the cupcakes danced around the table, their voices belting out a rap number —

"We're not sluts, tarts or strumpets. Bunnies, floozies or cock pockets. We are women, hear our roars! We are women, not cheap whores!"

The cupcakes suddenly stopped dancing. Cricket stepped forward and said, "Mister Mayor, we have a bone to pick with you."

"Bone? What bone?" he asked without a clue.

"We would like to negotiate payment for the movies we're making," Cricket stated. "We are professionals and should get a cut of each copy you sell. It may be porn to you, but it's our bread and butter."

The Mayor was visibly shaken. "Mmm, ma, movies? What movies?"

"The films we make for you at the Animal Bar."

Lusty "Ooooos" from the men.

"Films? What films?" The Mayor turned to the men and ordered, "Don't listen to this bimbo!"

Cricket shrugged. "Very well, your honor, you leave us no choice—"It's *showtime!*" She signaled to the State Safety Inspector (Exotica), who was positioned next to the huge TV screen on the wall.

"What are you doing?" the Mayor demanded to know.

"Showing one of your movies," Cricket explained. "It's rated 'G' for 'Genitalia'."

"You can't show that movie!" the Mayor gasped.

"Show the movie!" "Show the movie!" urged the men.

"I forbid you to show that movie!" yelled the Mayor.

"Okay," said Cricket. "how about you pay us for *not* showing the movie. Tit for tat."

The Mayor's eyes went shallow. "That's blackmail."

"Oh, no," corrected Brunhilda, "it is extortion."

"Und you vill pay, yah, for sure," Brunhelga declared.

The room thundered with men's voices—*"Show the movie!" "Show the movie!" "Show the movie!"*

"I will not allow you to show this movie!" the Mayor sputtered.

"Oh, I think you will," Cricket declared. as she and the Schnitzel Sisters unzipped their cupcakes, stepped out, fully-dressed, wielding automatic weapons. The rest of the well-armed Animal Girls joined them, taking aim at the men.

Cricket shouted. "Lights, camera, action!"

The images on the screen featured quick cuts of a naked Royal Bedwedder and members of the Men's Club making carnal whoopee with the Animal Girls.

The reaction was swift as the men turned on the Mayor.

"You been secretly filmin' us?"

"Usin' us to make a buck?"

"With our pee-pees hangin' out?"

"Yup," said Cricket, "Pricky and the twins in all their glory."

"Look, fellas," the Mayor fumbled, "this can all be explained..."

"Explain this!" Tempest cried out, as she shoved Royal's face into his spaghetti and yelled—"Food Fight!"

The men blitzed the Mayor!

The girls battered the men!

The men splattered the *Clowns*!

The *Clowns* launched a barrage!

Due to the unrelenting aroma of garlic the Men's Club was condemned.

The election was held. Sheriff Gus Clowndale soundly defeated Mongrel J. Clown who claimed the whole thing was rigged, but he was no longer worth listening to.

CHAPTER FIFTY THREE

Ron Rigler is back. He was released by the *New York Yankee* organization when he tested positive for "Somatotropin," a growth hormone used in raising livestock, and "Boldendone," an anabolic steroid used on horses.

Cisco Torcido gave up on Rigler, his parents disowned him, he's damaged goods. At the moment he's back in the *Clown* clubhouse, swallowing his pride.

Cookie approached Rigler and, in a soothing voice, told him, "Don't feel bad, Ron. You'll be back up there in no time. All it takes is stick-to-itive-ness…and don't get up you're sitting in Super Glue."

Rigler sprung up, leaving his ass on parade.

The boys pointed with mocking laughter. Rigler broke into tears.

"My, oh, my," Scraps mocked, "the lady's havin' a cryin' jag."

"Okay, boys, that's enough," Virgil drawled. "You had your fun. If you were glued to a bench it wouldn't be so funny, would it?"

Virgil placed a friendly hand on Rigler's shoulder and said, "You're gonna be okay, kid. I've seen a lotta hurlers and you're one'a the best. You can perform without a crutch. You just got to be willin' to give it a clean shot. You *are* willin', ain't ya?"

Rigler nodded and bawled like a baby.

The last three games of the season. My, how time flies.

We're hosting our archrival, the first place *Kickapoo Hayhaulers*. We have yet to win a game from this stellar organization, so it would give me great pleasure to wipe the smarm off their smirky faces.

The contest was about to begin. My players were tense. Our dugout felt like the tomb of the unknown ballplayer. Rabbi Melman decided to buck up his teammates with—"*Gray skies are gonna clear up, put on a happy face...!*"

He was pelted by baseball mitts.

I was going over the *Kickapoo* line-up with Doody when Doc Squeamish informed us she put Streamline on the disabled list. Doody told Virgil to warm up.

From her card table next to the dugout, Billie Bedwedder chattered into her microphone—"A huge howdy and hello to all you sports fans, and a very pleasant good afternoon wherever you may be. It's a beautiful day at historic Clowntown Memorial Stadium. The diamond glows like an emerald isle as our very own *Clowns* are about to face the dreaded *Kickapoo Hayhaulers*...But first a word from *Clownderson's Guns & Ammo*, where it's never too late for Christmas, there are a lot of nuts out there."

I handed the line-up card to our disgraced ex-Mayor and requested an invitation to next year's spaghetti bash. He zapped me a snarl and yelled—"*Play ball!*"

The fans yelled back—"*Up Yours!*"

Young Alice Anne, at the organ, blasted out "*Mary Had A Little Lamb!*" as the *Clowns* took the field.

The *Clowns* left the field to *Mozart's Requiem for the Dead*, as we got scrubbed by the Kickapoos 10-0. Virgil took the loss. Only gave up four hits. Try doing the math.

Game Two. I'm down to two starting pitchers and, with Streamline on the disabled list, I'll have to pitch Virgil on no-days rest.

More unwelcome news from Doc Squeamish. "Duke Rudolf has back spasms. Scraps Wisenheimer's migraine flared up. Iggy Fanoki has cramps and vomiting. Gives us six players in a nine player line-up."

I had no choice. "We'll have to forfeit."

Not so fast. Daddy O'Boy barged up to me, offering his sour sons to the team. Never one to quibble with a shotgun up my nose, I inserted his boys into the line-up.

And, in case you were wondering, Daddy's trio of sons dropped the ball, kicked the ball, couldn't hit the ball…

Virgil took another loss. No need to do the math.

CHAPTER FIFTY FOUR

Before game three Scraps told me chili peppers cured his migraine, Duke's spasms stopped spasming, but Iggy was suffering from restless bowel syndrome, leaving us one player short.

Leo Merkin, wearing his *Clown* uniform, appeared before me and announced, "I'm here to play and save the day."

I indulged him. "Okay, Sluggo, grab a bat and show me what you can do."

Leo rushed over, plucked a bat from the rack, tripped on the dugout step, and joined the disabled list with a twisted ankle.

My eyes scoured the dugout. Sitting in the corner was eighty-year-old Bob Snooks. "The team needs players and I'm here to help," he told me. "They used called me 'Swatman'!"

I sat next to Bob. "That's fine, Swat. But you know how you can help even more? Stay here on the bench. Show your support for the boys. It would mean a lot coming from an experienced athlete like you."

"Glad to be of service," he grinned.

Peewee took me aside. "Mister McKay," he said, "I'm ready to take over for Iggy in center. I roam the outfield like Spiderman, and being a murderer it's the least I can do."

I thought about Peewee's offer, figured why not? Peewee could be a weapon. At four feet tall, he has no strike zone, so he'll walk all the time.

It's like when Bill Veeck, owner of the *St. Louis Browns,* put three-foot-seven Eddie Gaedel up to bat. His uniform number was "1/8." And, you guessed it, Eddie walked.

My advice to Peewee was, "When you get up to bat, don't swing. Just wait. You'll get on base."

Peewee's eyes beamed like headlights as he scooped up his glove and flew out to shag fly balls.

Max Doody snuck over to me and whispered..."Don't tell the boys, but the *Chicago Cub* scout is here."

"A *Cub* scout is actually *here?!*" I blurted.

Doody clapped his hand over my mouth. "Shhhh! Not so loud." He looked around to ensure no one was listening. "There's more. The *Milwaukee Brewers* are here, too."

"But I never talked to the *Brewers.*"

"You didn't hafta," Doody explained. "They heard the *Cubs* were gonna be scoutin' the *Hayhaulers,* so they're here to beat 'em to it, and we're here to beat the *Hayhaulers* 'cause our boys are gonna show those scouts what kinda shit we're made of."

I looked over to where the *Hayhauler's* 6-9, 240 pound ace, Moe Rinker, was warming up. Blazing fastball, wicked slider, he'd flatten his grandmother if she crowded the plate.

Heinie Pratt appeared in full uniform, "Goddamn *Kickashit Noballers,*" he grumbled, "Think they can walk their spikes all over us. Well, no siree, not while I'm managin' this here ballclub!"

Heinie lumbered onto the field, snatched-up the garden hose, and soaked the entire *Kickapoo* dugout!

Their manager, Snide Shirker, screamed obscenities at Heinie— "!&%#*^%#@%^!"

Heinie screamed back—"!&**$@^%#!^&%*%*%!!"

I ran out on the field, tried to wrestle the hose from Heinie. In the struggle we both sprayed the Kickapoo dugout!

"%!!o&%$!@#)*&^%!%&%#@$*!#@&!!%!!!"

Doc Squeamish ran up and wrenched the hose from our grips, saying— "Look what you've done, Heinie. Gone and made those *Kickapoos* mad. Honestly, I just don't know what I'm going to do with you."

Heinie was humbled, and said, "Geez, Edna, I was just havin' fun."

Doc was sweetly stern. "Fun is not threatening to drown people, my love. Now, get back to our dugout, lock your mouth and throw away the key."

"Aw, do I have to?" Heinie pouted.

"I won't make fudge," she threatened.

Heinie locked his mouth and threw away the key.

Doc Squeamish turned her attention to me. "Now, what's this I hear about you starting Streamline West?"

"He says he's good to go."

"That's because he sees his injury as a temporary obstacle. It's unmanly to show weakness. To endure pain is courageous. It's all a bunch of hooey. Rest is the only way to recovery."

"That's what I told him. But there are scouts here from the *Chicago Cubs* and the *Milwaukee Brewers*. This is Streamline's big chance. Maybe his only chance."

Doc understood. "Keep him on a short leash."

CHAPTER FIFTY FIVE

Ex-Mayor Clown, called—*"Play Ball!"* and was attacked by a cascade of women's panties. This gave me time for a last-minute pep talk.

"Okay, boys, let's face it," I began, "we're the underdogs. David versus Goliath. But David *beat* Goliath because Goliath underestimated David just like those *Kickapoos* are underestimating you, selling you short, taking you for granted...Well, fellas, this is an opening. An opportunity. A chance for you to defeat fear with confidence. To show the world you will never stop trying, because trying leads to excellence, and excellence is your ticket to success!"

There were "yays!" and a few "yahoos!"

Scraps gave me a nudge. "That was a pretty good speech, McKay. Which movie is it from?"

"No movie," I said. "Just me, Lombardi, a dash of Ditka."

The field was cleared of panties, the game got underway.

Top of the first, Streamline struck out the side. Bottom of the first, Allstate led off with a bunt single, stole second, snatched third, hijacked home, we pulled ahead 1-0.

In our half of the second, Noodles greeted Moe Rinker's fastball with a three-run homer!

Streamline was on top of his game, pitching four shutout innings with the score, *Clowns*—4, *Kickapoos*—0.

Bottom of the fourth. I reminded Peewee of our "walk" strategy. Peewee strolled up to the plate and lashed a screaming double against the outfield wall. Scraps banged-out a single, scoring Peewee. 5-zip!

Sixth inning. Streamline still shutting out the *Kickapoos*...Then a single, a walk, another single loaded the bases with two outs.

Streamline let go with a slider to *Kickapoo* third baseman Bonzo Moretti. Moretti smashed a long drive—back, back, back—!

Rabbi Urban Melman *crashed* into the outfield wall, making a spectacular catch to snuff out a rally! He stumbled back to the bench, told Doc there was something wrong with his eye. Doc rushed him off for an exam.

Seventh inning. *Kickapoos* coming up to bat. Doody nudged me and asked, "Whaddya know about playin' the outfield?"

"Played a little in high school," I said.

"Good," said Doody, "you're our right fielder."

The fact is I played very little in high school, so scared silly and somewhat fired-up, I dashed into the clubhouse to get my glove.

I overheard voices. Noodles and his father were in hushed conversation and, being a hopeless curiotic, I had no choice but to listen in.

"So, you're planning to stick around?" asked Warren.

"Yeah," said Noodles, "I really think I could have career in baseball."

"You're taking a big chance."

"But people say I'm Major League," Noodles said with conviction.

"What about our project?"

"Nah, acting's not my game."

"And the girl?"

"I love her, Warren, with all my heart."

"Okay, have it your way," Warren sighed, "I'm heading home to L.A. Got a script due at Warners."

"Stay for the wedding," said Noodles. "Be my best man."

"Sure," Warren agreed, "what's a big brother for?"

CHAPTER FIFTY SIX

So there I was, positioned in right field, questions hammering my brain —
 What kind of a "project" were Noodles and Warren talking about?
 What does "acting" have to do with it?
 And what the hell kind of father is his son's "big brother?"
 Home to L.A? Warren told me he taught science to fat-headed gnomes in Connersville, Indiana. L. A. can't hope to live up to Connersville.
 Warren said he has a script due at Warners. Sounds like writer talk to me. Could he be…? Yes…He's that guy I used to see at Writers Guild meetings.
 I was so captivated by my thoughts I failed to catch the ball that fell in front of me. By the time I picked it up and lobbed a throw to the infield, there was a *Kickapoo* on third.
 The next batter hit a scorching line drive. I took off, glove held high, caught it with my eyes shut and all was forgiven.

 Eighth inning. Streamline West still working on a shut-out. The *Kickapoos* looked disoriented. They're not used to losing. Major League scouts are watching.
 The ugly incident began in the bottom of the eighth when Scraps Wisenheimer crowded the plate and Moe Rinker zapped a fastball that

just missed his head. Scraps yelled out to Rinker—*"Do that again and you'll be eatin' this bat!"*

"Naw," volleyed Rinker, *"I'll be eatin' your mother!"*

Scraps charged the mound and belted Rinker! Rinker returned the belt! And, for some reason I won't get into, our bus driver, Grinny, had replaced Billie at the microphone and was doing the play-by-play—"Holy wrath of Khan! Both benches have cleared and players are goin' boldly where no men have gone before! Our *Clowns* are all over those *Kickapoos*, giving them all they've got! What a ruckus! Go *Clowns*, go! Live long and prosper...!"

Civilization was temporarily restored when I told *the Hayhaulers* manager, Snide Shirker, my *Clowns* were willing to call it a game and go home with a victory. Shirker jammed his fleshy nose into mine and told me to, *"Get ready for a shellackin'!"*

The shellackin' began in top of the ninth when Streamline gave up a home run to *Kickapoo* right fielder Johnny Mayhem. Score 5-1. Streamline responded with two outs, followed by two walks.

Kickapoo left fielder, Bulldog Spink, tossed away three of the four bats he was swinging and stepped up to the plate. He ran the count to 3 and 2. A strike in the dirt got past Stubby Jenks. Bases loaded. Next batter, *Kickapoo's* menacing first baseman, Knocko Welch.

Stubby called for conference. I joined Spook and Doody on the mound.

Stubby told Streamline to, "Stop shaking off my signs and tell me what you wanna throw the guy."

"If it's all the same to you," said Streamline, "I'll just hold onto the ball."

Stubby shook his head. "I don't think they'll let you do that."

"Let's just wait a while," Streamline shrugged. "Maybe Knocko will get bored and quit baseball."

Figuring my pitcher needed a jolt of confidence, I stepped in. "Streamline," I said, "there's not a thing for you to worry about. With that blazing fastball of yours Knocko doesn't have a chance."

Somewhat encouraged, and realizing he had a job to do, Streamline pulled himself together and hurled a blazing fastball to the plate.

Knocko knocked it into the next county. All tied at 5-5.

Stubby signaled for another conference on the mound where I apologized for my misguided jolt of confidence.

Doc Squeamish joined us, asked Streamline about his shoulder. "Shoulder feels fine," he replied, "but I think I dislocated my thumb in the brawl."

Doc swept Streamline away for an exam. Doody called for Ron Rigler to take the mound in relief, but no Rigler. We found him napping in the corner of the clubhouse, smelling like a brewery and speaking in tongues.

Spook told Virgil Weathers to warm up, but Virgil was tired, erratic, couldn't throw strikes.

I spotted this new kid throwing smoke on the sideline, walked over for a closer look and asked, "What's your name, young man?"

"Fireball Ferguson," said Billie Bedwedder, wearing her false beard and mustache.

"Billie, what do you think you're doing?"

"It's do or die, boss," she crisply stated. "Put me in. My fastball's a real nipper today."

"I can't put you in, it's against the rules."

"So is playing ball without a pitcher."

That didn't take long to sink in. "Now pitching for the *Clowns*—Fireball Ferguson!"

Billie took the mound. Three nippy fastballs retired the side.

Top of the tenth. Still knotted at 5-5. *Kickapoo* shortstop Tony Testeroni singled with two outs. He took a big lead at first. Billie whipped the ball to Cookie. Testeroni dove back—*safe!*

Testeroni continued to harass Billie, taking big leads and making her throw to first. Billie signaled for the infielders to join her on the mound. They huddled for a moment, returned to their positions.

Testeroni took another big lead. Cookie removed the ball from his glove and tagged Testeroni *out!* How about that, fans? The "hidden ball" trick still works!

Bottom of the tenth, still tied, two outs. Scraps Wisenheimer swung and missed the first two pitches. In frustration he turned around, swung at the catcher, missed again, and was ejected from the game.

Bob Snooks hustled over to me and said, "Don't bother to ask, you need a pinch-hitter and I'm all you got." He grabbed a bat, stood at the top of the dugout and bellowed to the fans—"*Now batting for the Clowns, "Swatman Bob Snooks!"*

Snooks ambled out to the batter's box, ready to face *Kickapoo* reliever Walgreen Fernandez. He ran the count to three and two. Fouled off six pitches. Yelled out to Fernandez—*"Hey, young fella, throw me somethin' I can hit!"*

Fernandez whipped a fastball down the middle. Snooks connected—back, back, back—*out'a here!*

Snooks rounded the bases, tipping his hat to the rollicking crowd. He dove headfirst into home plate with the winning run and was mobbed by his teammates. He shot me a wink and said, "That ball's headed for Saint Pete's birdbath."

CHAPTER FIFTY SEVEN

The clubhouse rocked! *Clowns* doused each other with the garden hose, then drenched our hero, Swatman Snooks, who took it in with a dopey grin.

Word got around that scouts from the *Cubs* and *Brewers* saw the game and my boys were filled with anticipation. Any minute now those scouts were gonna come in with big contracts and huge signing bonuses…Yup, any minute now…any minute…

…So, where are the scouts? Why aren't they here? Didn't they like us? They didn't like us. They hated us. We're no good. We suck!

Time to rally. "Okay, boys," I said, "you were all superb out there today. You ended your season on a positive note. You played at your highest level, beat the toughest team, and the scouts saw that. But don't expect them to walk right in here. There's a system, a procedure they have to follow. Things like this take time."

A *Milwaukee Brewers* cap appeared at the door. "Excuse me," said the man under the cap, "I'm looking for one of your players."

Allstate slid headfirst between the man's legs!

The man consulted his clipboard. "His name is, uh…"

Breaths were held as each *Clown* waited to hear his name.

"…Fireball Ferguson," the man announced. "The boy who closed today's game."

"That's what he said his name was," offered Spook. "He all of a sudden showed up from nowhere. I looked for him after the game and all I found was this phony beard and mustache." He held them up. "The boy must have wanted to look older."

The scout handed me his card. "Tell Fireball the *Brewers* are interested."

A lingering silence.

Cookie spoke up. "Someday somebody will get interested in me. It will happen. The Lord listens in strange ways."

"I'm twenty-nine," Stubby sighed. "Next birthday I'll be over-the-hill."

"They got tryout camps all over," stated Iggy. "I'll catch on, just you wait and see."

"I think I'll hitchhike to Mexico," said Scraps, "hook up with a team. Maybe teach English."

"Well, I'm not letting this get me down," said Streamline. "I will continue to work hard, I will get better, I will never be a never-was."

Duke slammed his duffel on the floor, saying, "How many worthless years does it take to make it in this friggin' game? If I was smart I'd go back to Boston. Practice law. I know how personal injury feels."

Ron Rigler tipsily rose from his chair to address the group. "Ladies and gentleclowns," he slurred, "My apologies for bein' drunk and an asshole, it's tough dealin' with the pressure, but that's all over, end of story. I am not letting me beat me, gonna kick this thing...and that's all I have to say on the subject. Goodbye, good riddance, fuck off."

Having apologized, Rigler passed out.

Noodles burst into the clubhouse, all excited. "The *Chicago Cubs* want me!" he exclaimed. "They're talking Double-A! Two steps from the bigs! Isn't it great?"

After a bleak silence, Noodles asked, "You guys aren't mad at me, are you?"

The team rose as one and soaked Noodles with the garden hose.

Noodles shook himself dry and shouted—"Everybody to the Big Rack Lounge—the drinks are on *me!*"

The room emptied in a plume of smoke.

Doc Squeamish took me aside. "Rabbi Melman suffered a severe blow to the eye which detached his retina. The ambulance rushed him up to the Eye Center of Clam Falls for outpatient surgery. I'm driving up right now to pick him up."

Peewee breezed up to me, all grins. "Mister McKay," he exclaimed, "the *Chicago Cub* scout made me promise I'd call him when I'm sixteen!"

CHAPTER FIFTY EIGHT

Back in my room I Googled the Writers Guild of America membership site. No listing for a Warren Weaver. There's a Warren Farnum. He could've changed it. If my last name was Farzock I'd be a Farnum. And if Warren is a Farnum that would make Noodles a Farnum. Warren said they were family, referred to Noodles as "bro'. Maybe Tinky had two sons who both hated his guts.

A rapping at my door. Rabbi Irving Melman stood there, staring at the ground. "Hullo," he muttered. "I'm back."

He walked in, still staring at the ground. "Everything's okay with me, how about you?"

"I'm good. I take it the operation went well?"

"Oh, fine, I'll be fine," he said. "You think the *Cubs* could use a one-eyed outfielder?"

I leaned down, saw he was wearing a huge bandage over his right eye.

"I have to keep my face down for several weeks," he explained. "After that my eye will be almost as good as new, meaning it's time to move on. There's a temple in Brooklyn looking for an assistant rabbi to coordinate youth activities, coach the baseball team. Wouldn't it be great if one of my boys played in Yankee Stadium?"

I devised a plan to solve the case. The wedding ceremony was scheduled for one o'clock. Gave me time to prepare.

I bought some clown make-up at Clownworth's Five & Dime, then stealthily crept into the deserted town square and removed the clown costume from the Nutty statue. I knew the citizens of Clowntown would be dazzled to see a naked Nutty, but justice had to be served.

"No way!" was Leo's quick reply. "I am not gonna dress up like a Clown."

"You told me you were born to be a clown."

"It was a silly dream."

I pushed the costume at him. "After all the trouble you went to dig up and clean the costume the least you can do is wear it."

"No," he pushed back. "It still smells like crotch"

"Leo, Leo, Leo," I sighed, "I think you're underestimating your skills as a performer. You're a wonderful actor. You were a smash as the dead body in our school play. Not once did you breathe. Everyone thought you were dead. It's time you shared your talent with the world."

Leo's face lit up like Broadway. "You really think I'm a wonderful actor?"

"You have a gift," I said. "You're not afraid to show your dopey side."

"It's a family trait," he beamed.

I worked at full-speed transforming Leo Merkin into the spitting image of Nutty Nuckleball. Having finished, I stood back to admire my work.

"Leo," I asked, "is that you in there?"

"Shhhhh!" he hushed. "I'm channeling my inner clown."

Now in case you're wondering why I was bringing Nutty back to life, it gets back to what I overheard in the clubhouse…Warren mentioned something about a "project." Noodles said "acting" wasn't for him. Warren told Noodles he was "taking a big chance sticking around." The clincher was when Warren called himself Noodles' "big brother."

…So, piecing these pieces of the puzzle together I have concluded that Noodles and Warren are Tinky's sons who were out to wreak revenge on their father who was abusive to their mother, putting her through a slow mental torture, ultimately causing her death.

And, consider this. Warren is a writer. This murder could've been a scripted reality show. The brothers knew their estranged father was doing his clown act on the ballpark circuit, knew he'd be in Clowntown, and plotted his demise.

The Farzock brothers are going to come unglued when daddy returns to haunt them.

CHAPTER FIFTY NINE

Clown Memorial Stadium. The wedding of Cricket and Noodles.

Before the ceremony I ran into Noodles and Warren in the clubhouse and figured why wait? This was the perfect time to confront them and nail down the truth.

"Hey, guys, got a minute?" I casually asked.

"Sure, sure" said Warren, "what's up?"

"Oh, I think you know."

"Know what?"

"You can stop pretending."

"About what?" asked Noodles.

"About the fact that you're not who you say you are."

Warren was quick to protest. "What the hell are you talking about?"

"Don't play coy with me, Warren. I know the truth. You're a writer and your brother here is an actor."

A lengthy pause...Noodles finally said, "How did you find out?"

"I've been known to play detective from time to time. I also happen to know that...(dramatic pause)...*You are the sons of Tinky Farzock!*"

After an empty silence, Noodles asked..."Who's Tinky Farzock?"

"Your father!"

"Our father's name is Chuck and he lives in Arizona." said Warren.

"Very funny," I laughingly dismissed. "Now try telling the truth."

"Okay," said Warren, "You want the truth, here's the truth. Our last name isn't Weaver, it's Farnum, and, yes, we are brothers."

"We took on the identities of the characters in our screenplay," Noodles added.

"Your screenplay...?"

"Yeah, we've been doing research," Warren explained, "sort of improvising a script. We figured if we were going to make a movie about small-time baseball we should immerse ourselves in small-time baseball."

"A movie? You're making a movie?"

"That was our plan," said Warren, "I'd direct and play the father and my brother would star as my son until he decided to get married and have a glorious future in baseball."

"I told Cricket the whole story," said Noodles. "She's on my side."

Warren placed a friendly hand on my shoulder. "Look, McKay, we're fellow writers. We protect each other, right?"

"Someone has to."

"Absolutely," Warren acknowledged, "So don't go talking about this to anybody. When people know you're a filmmaker, they start auditioning."

I stood there with egg on my face.

...Or maybe not. Do these two guys really expect me to believe what I just heard? Was I just handed a load of bullshit? How will they act when they see their father come back to life?

The wedding ceremony was about to begin. A fingernail poked my butt. I whipped around to see Luscious O'Boy in an octopus-print gown. "Springer, my love," she hushed, "we can no longer be engaged, I am in love with another."

"Really? That's *terrific!*" I exclaimed, then was quick to grim-up..."I mean, wow, what a disappointment. Who's the lucky guy?"

"Exotica. She promised she'd become the man she really is."

Luscious pasted me a kiss and flounced off saying, "Daddy's gonna crap his pants when I tell him!"

My eyes were drawn to Tempest Bedwedder looking top-notch in an orange dress with purple piping. She blew me a kiss. I caught it, blew it back.

Alice Anne plunked out the Wedding March. The *Clowntown Clowns* formed an "arch" with their bats. The bride and groom took their places at home plate, Noodles in his baseball uniform, Cricket all sultry in a leopard-skin sarong.

Warren stood as best man. Tempest, matron of honor. The Animal Girls, dressed in their uninhibited best, gathered around toting buckets of rice.

Rabbi Melman stared face-down at home plate, ready to begin the ceremony. "I'm a smidge nervous," he murmured to the ground. "This is my first wedding, wish me luck." He composed himself and began, "We are gathered here today..."

"*I can't hear you!*" Royal's voice heckled from the stands.

"*We are gathered here today...!*" Rabbi shouted.

Where the hell is Leo? I thought to myself. Nutty is supposed to come out and prance around before the wedding starts and the wedding has started!

Rabbi continued shouting "*...to witness the joining of Cricket and Noodles...!*"

"*Hold on!*" a voice yelled out. "*Don't start without us!*"

Doctor Edna Squeamish, her silvery hair twirled like soft serve, led Heinie Pratt up to home plate. He looked spiffy in his newly-laundered *Clown* uniform. Doc was picture-perfect in a yellowed wedding dress reeking of mothballs.

"Me'n the little lady are gettin' hitched," Heinie announced.

"That's right," added Doc, "big boy and I wish to become one."

This caused a happy stir as places were taken and Rabbi Melman started over. "Dearly beloved, we are gathered here today to join these four souls in matrimony because love is a many-splendored thing, or as the *Beatles* once observed—"*All you need is love, da-da-da-da-da...!*"

Rabbi sang the entire song, then segued to—"Do you Cricket and Noodles and Edna and Heinie take the opposite other to be your husbands and wives, promising to love, honor cherish, and seek together a life honored by the faith of Israel?"

The four of them "I doed," leaving me to wonder if Rabbi Melman just converted them to Judaism.

A duck call *pierced* the air! Leo, as Nutty Nuckleball, scooted onto the field dragging his four-foot glove and oversized bat. He tripped over his floppy shoes, did a pratfall, got up, rubbed dirt on his hands and under his arms, spit water in the air, it landed on his face...

As Leo performed, I studied Warren and Noodles to see if they would finally reveal themselves to be guilty.

They thought Nutty was a laugh riot!

"*I hate clowns!*" Heinie squawked as he grabbed the garden hose and brought Leo's performance to a soggy end.

Mayor Gus Clowndale showed up to retrieve Nutty's uniform. "The citizens are in quite a flurry over Nutty's state of undress," he said. "His wilted winky is all over Facebook."

CHAPTER SIXTY

The wedding reception was held at the Bed & Barn barn and, whilst quaffing a brew, Billie Bedwedder came up and said, "In less insane times I would have considered the *Milwaukee Brewers*' offer, but they'd wonder why I never took a shower. So, knowing this might be the case, I sent tapes of my broadcasts to potential sponsors, and the New Glarus Brewery, makers of Spotted Cow and Fat Squirrel, offered me a job as the announcing voice of the *Class A Pirate City Smugglers*. From there, I will rise up to the major leagues, pay off the mortgage on our house, and boot Royal Bedwedder out of my life. Dorks don't deserve to be dads."

She pecked me on the cheek and said, "Thanks for not laughing at me."

Daddy O'Boy was suddenly in my face. "Caught ya, ya slippery snivelin' snake, ya slimy skunkball, ya scummy scuzzy stinkbag…"

"Is there a problem?" I inquired.

"It's yew!" Daddy roared. "Fuckin' with my darlin' daughter's head, turnin' her into a tit-suckin' lesbo! I'm her daddy, that's my job." His rifle lifted my chin. "I knowed I should'a killed ya when I first met ya and now yer gonna *die!*"

Tempest appeared next to Daddy, snatched his weapon—"Gimme that thing! Nobody's hurtin' my man."

Royal Bedwedder roared up to Tempest. "Piss off, you cheatin' whore!"

Tempest threw her arms around my neck. "Sorry, Royal, I am in love with this man and there's nothing you can do about it!"

I eased her away—"What's say we all discuss this like rational human beings..."

"Shut your hole, you Hollywood housewrecker," snarled Royal.

"I'm having a fling, Royal," Tempest continued to dig. "You know what a fling is. You've been flinging all over town!"

Royal pointed an accusing finger at me—"Now, see what you done, McKay? Went and put the devil in my woman. You been askin' for trouble ever since you showed up and it's time I did somethin' about that."

A group of men gathered around Royal. He turned to them and ordered—"Okay, boys, let's *get* him!"

They cocked their weapons and made their way toward me, homicide in their hearts.

CHAPTER SIXTY ONE

So that's how I happened to be dashing through the woods, pursued by a bloodthirsty mob out to kill me. It's amazing how violence brings people together.

I turned to see ex-Mayor Clown running alongside me. "What are you doing here?" I huffed.

"Getting even, McKay," he puffed. "You wrecked my life and now you're going to pay for it."

"Great Bogart," I acknowledged. "Now do Cagney."

He ignored my request. "The Minneheehaw Tribe paid me a visit last night," he panted. "They heard I was going to build on my land. The land you sold me. The land I own that you never owned. My land that is *their* land! What do you have to say about that?"

"Real estate has its quirks."

"This is no joke, McKay," he gasped. "You have whipped up the brains of my hookers, making them do unspeakable things against me. You caused me to lose the faith of the rabble and robbed me of my prestige."

"But I have a plan," he continued, "a way to get the citizens of Clowntown back on my side. A way to be their champion once again."

He skidded us to a stop, shouted back to the approaching mob—*"McKay's over here, boys! Come and get him!"*

Mumbly voices closed in. I was surrounded by yappy dogs with drippy fangs. Thinking quickly I sang—"*Who Let the Dogs Out, Woof, Woof...!*" The dogs just stared at me. Everyone's a critic.

I pointed to Mongrel J. Clown and told the dogs, "See this man? He's the bad guy."

The dogs took off after the terrified ex-Mayor!

I heard a whispered voice..."Hey, chief, over here."

It was Scraps Wisenheimer. "Follow me," he said, "I know where you can hide."

A cave. *"Dank"* pretty well describes it. Hieroglyphics on the wall told me: *Wanda wears falsies. Batman's a queer. For a good time call...*Someone scribbled out the number. So much for a good time.

"This is my private place," Scraps explained. "I come here to think about life and shit like that...Like I was thinkin' about that stunt where you brought back Nutty. That was your idea, right?"

"Yeah, I resurrected him."

"Think you're pretty clever, dont'cha?" he said. "Well, it is very unrespectful to bring a dead person back to life no matter how rotten he was...So, what tipped ya off?"

"About what?" I wondered.

"That Nutty was my dad."

It took a moment to absorb this..."But you said your dad died before you were born."

"He was dead in my eyes," Scraps sneered. "Always beatin' up on me, and mom would see it, and get out'a control with her cryin'. She was a good person, a kind person...he put her through hell."

Scraps rambled on. "One time when I was nine, he got home from drinkin' and him and mom had an argument, and he grabbed me and held a knife to my throat. Threatened to *kill* me. Just to win an argument. And mom, poor mom, she got all afraid and frantic and her heart...it gave out." Tears streamed down his cheeks..."Wisenheimer was her maiden name. Now it's mine."

He wiped away the tears, collected himself. "You wanna know how I did it? I went online. Scored me some curare', a dart, and a blowgun. Got the idea from an old Charlie Chan movie on TV...And I got lucky. When that dart hit my dad I saw him snatch it from his neck, and throw it away, and fans were runnin' all over the field, so nobody saw me run out and pick up the dart."

"Then y'know what I did?" he said, "I sold the dart and the blowgun on eBay and stashed the poison bottle in the old garage in a bag of peas so no one would ever find it."

He clutched his head with his hands and cried out, "*Geezus—these headaches are killin' me.*"

"Scraps, listen," I said, "you need help. I'll call Doc Squeamish."

He shook his head. "Uh-uh, can't do that, ain't too sure about that. Now that ya know the truth, you'll hafta turn me in, which means I can't let ya do that." He pulled out a small handgun, pointed it my way.

Tempest suddenly appeared, dressed in a blaze orange cap and jumpsuit. She pointed to Scraps—"What's that toy gun you're holding? Why, it's an Apache revolver! Knife, brass knuckles, revolver all in one. Flimsy, inaccurate, probably the worst handgun ever made. Sure the brass knuckles might work, but the knife is where the barrel should be, meaning there is no barrel, meaning it could blow up in your face, and who wants a barbecued nose?"

She whipped out a sleek, shiny handgun, aimed it at Scraps. "My Glock 19, on the other hand, is a far superior weapon. Powerful, reliable, used by the FBI, the CIA, and James Bond."

She reached for Scraps' revolver. He jumped back—fired! Nothing. Fired again!! More nothing.

Scraps dropped the gun, clutched his head and screamed—"*It hurts! Make it stop hurting...*" He shuddered and fell unconscious.

I heard moblike voices. "The nuts are closing in, let's blow this pop stand."

"Follow me," said Tempest. "I parked your car by the road."

I scooped up Scraps' limp body and took refuge in Wolfgang.

The mob spotted us and opened fire!

Tempest gunned us into action!

CHAPTER SIXTY TWO

Tempest roared Wolfgang down the road. I'm in back, eye on Scraps, still out cold.

"The inmates are on the warpath again," she observed. "Won't be the first time a decent man was run out of town."

"Thanks for bailing me out."

"It was the heroic thing to do."

"How the hell did you find me?"

"Strategic thinking," she explained. "The main road runs alongside the woods and, since my car is in the shop, I hot-wired yours and tracked you and the mob on Google Earth. I'm resourceful that way. It's one of my outstanding qualities."

We dropped Scraps at Mayor Clowndale's office. I called Doc Squeamish, she's on her way.

Tempest barreled Wolfgang down Main Street. Time was short. I had to get to the Bed & Barn, pick up Leo, and high-tail out of town before my funeral got underway.

I saw the dogs chase Mongrel J. Clown down the street, through the town square, knocking over the Nutty statue, killing Tinky all over again.

Tempest suddenly screeched Wolfgang to a stop!

"Why are you stopping?" I blurted. "The Bed & Barn is five blocks up."

"Okay, here's the deal," she explained. "The girls and me, we knew the bozos were out to get you, so we worked out a plan. It's brilliant, you'll love it. The school bus should be here any minute now."

"Bus?" I asked in confusion. "People are out to massacre me and I'm waiting for a school bus?"

"Part of our plan," she explained. "Me and the girls disabled all their vehicles, and the only thing that works is the bus."

"I have a better plan," I told her. "Let's flee for my life."

"Nope, can't do it yet. Gotta wait till they see us."

I heard the chugging of the school bus in the distance. It came into view, packed with the frenzied mob, Royal Bedwedder at the wheel.

Tempest jumped out of Wolfgang, whipped a finger at the oncoming bus and shouted—*"Hey, pansy-asses! Come and get him!"*

The pansy-asses fired their weapons! Bullets pierced Wolfgang!

Tempest dove back into the car and peeled us off, saying—"Sorry about the bullets. Insurance might cover it."

Tempest sped Wolfgang toward Clown Lake—then abruptly hit the brakes to reduce our speed.

"Why are we slowing down?" I thought I should know.

"So the bus can catch us."

"That may not be the best idea."

"You'll see."

What I saw was the school bus catching up to us as we headed toward the Clown Lake pier!

Ahead of us, lined on the side of the road, were Cricket, Luscious, Exotica, Chastity, Destiny, the Schnitzel sisters, and Cloris, the bowlegged contortionist—all provocatively posing in the nude.

Tempest gave them a thumbs up as we passed. They flipped their nipples in response.

Tempest hit the accelerator—headed directly for the pier—the bus close behind.

She yanked a hard left away from the pier!

Royal, hypnotized by flipping nipples, flew the bus off the pier with a titanic splash!

The dogs chased Mongrel J. Clown into view! Then stopped to enjoy his screaming belly flop!

Tempest screeched Wolfgang to a halt, turned to me with a satisfied grin and said, "This ought'a get us ladies some respect."

I watched as a police rescue team pulled ex-Mayor Clown and the mob from the lake and arrested them for disturbing the peace.

Tempest turned to me, had something important to say. "Springer, thanks to you I now know what it's like to be in love. And I would really like to run away with you to L.A. and lead a glamorous life, but the idea of starting over in a big city scares the living shit out of me. I've gotta take time to think about what I am and who I want to be. I'm finally gonna move me and my daughter out of that house, get a little place, re-build my life here in Clowntown."

She went on. "I want to help those girls at the bar grow and reach their full potential, There's a lot more to them than tits and ass, even though they came in handy today."

She extended her hand. "Springer McKay, it's been a total treat to know you. Best orgasm ever. A real moonshot!"

CHAPTER SIXTY THREE

Okay, I'm not a professional detective. I got the part right about a son killing his father for killing his mother. I do the best I can in these circumstances. I can't help it if murder shows up wherever I go.

So, that was that. Season over. In the clubhouse, my boys were packing up for uncertain futures.

Cookie Calaboosa came up to me and confided, "God spoke to me."

"What was he wearing?" I wondered.

"A halo. He told me to finish high school."

"God gives good advice."

"Yeah. God's smart that way."

Iggy Fanoki joined in. "Me? I'm quittin' baseball. Goin' into the plumbin' game. Gonna make somethin' of myself, you wait and see."…He paused for a minute, tears welled his eyes. "I was a good ballplayer, wasn't I, Mister McKay?"

"Yeah, Igg," I said. "A real pro."

Duke Rudolf whacked my back. "Well, McKay. I'm off to Boston to practice law. If you ever get a whiplash give me a call."

Allstate Cabrera pumped my hand, rattled-off something in Spanish. Duke translated. "He says you are a fine Hollywood man, and wishes you good luck marrying movie stars."

Streamline West took me aside. "A scout from the *Texas Rangers* was here," he excitedly disclosed. "Offered me a five-thousand-dollar signing bonus. Told me I'd be assigned to the *Class A California League*. Make about a grand a week. After deductions for housing, taxes and stuff, I'll take home about two-fifty, but it's *real* baseball. My chance to go all the way."

"I believe you will."

There were tearful farewells, phone numbers were exchanged, I urged everyone to keep in touch.

Max Doody bid me goodbye and walked off, muttering to himself... "Well, Doody, looks like it's the end of the road for you. Why? Whaddya mean why? Nobody wants a guy with nowhere to go. You had your glory days, saved some bucks. Think I'll buy a Waterpik. Save the teeth I still got..." He removed the chaw from his mouth and dropped it in the garbage can, saying, "This stuff'll kill ya."

Spook Spindler approached "Perhaps I could interest you in *Gladiator*, a brand new hair enhancer from the wonderful people at *Rightway*. Swipes away the grey in one sweet swoop."

"I like my grey hair."

"It puts ten years on you."

"That's not gonna work this time."

"If I sell three more bottles I win a trip to Aruba."

I bought three bottles.

Leo waddled up, all smiles. "I'll bet you didn't think I had a head for business?"

"It never entered my mind."

"Well, it has now." he proudly stated. "Now that the Minneheehaw Tribe owns the team, I figured they might be in need my services, so we pow-wowed and you are now looking at the new Nutty Nuckleball!"

Leo blasted his duck call, fell on his ass, and is back on the disabled list.

CHAPTER SIXTY FOUR

So here I am, back in Tinseltown, hoping for a writing gig so I can stay relevant. On my return, Ralph Dalton Futz presented me with his bill. I set up a payment program.

Tempest and I have become pen pals. She sends me the latest Clowntown buzz.

Billie's broadcasting career caught fire. ESPN is scouting her.

Cricket Monsoon-Farnum earned a scholarship to Northwestern University where she will major in finance.

The Schnitzel Sisters are starring in a new reality show---*The Real Housewives of Milwaukee*.

Bob Snooks is the new manager of the *Clowntown Clowns*.

Doc Squeamish is taking good care of Heinie. She says the guy still hits the long ball.

Biggest news of all, Allstate Cabrera got Cloris, the bow-legged contortionist pregnant, and he is staying in Clowntown to be a good husband and father. Love conquers baseball.

I hear from the guys now and then.

Virgil Weathers is back with his wife and kids and making big bucks in recreational marijuana.

Irving Melman is the assistant rabbi at a reform synagogue in Brooklyn. His team, the *Mighty Maccabees*, will be competing in the *Little League World Series* at Yankee Stadium.

Max Doody moved to a retirement community in Santa Fe, New Mexico where his armed Venus's and leggy mermaids sell at astronomical prices.

Spook Spindler writes that he never left Aruba, and is the starting pitcher for the *Oranjestad Oranges* of the Amsterdam League.

Stubby Jenks wandered into a tryout camp. Walked away with a contract to play in Japan, and is the father of twin daughters named Suki and Yaki. I couldn't make this up.

The media fills me in on the rest.

Streamline West's arm got worse, but the *Texas Ranger organization* never lost faith in their prospect and paid for Tommy John surgery. Streamline's first Major League game was a shut-out.

Cookie Calaboosa played brilliantly for his school team. He sprouted from five-foot-six to six-foot-two, and *Sports Illustrated* projects him as the future first baseman for the *Boston Red Sox*.

Noodles Farnum, leftfielder for the *Chicago Cubs*, is leading the Majors in homers. His brother, Warren, is his agent.

Ron Rigler became the host of *Take My Spouse!*, a TV reality show that pits married couples against each other to see who can cheat without being found out. Ron got sued for sexual harassment.

A trial was held in Clowntown, Wisconsin. Scraps Wisenheimer appeared with his attorney, Clyde Burning Bush, who convinced a jury that Wilbur "Scraps" Wisenheimer, due to repeated blows to the head, had suffered traumatic brain injury and was legally insane at the time of the murder. Scraps was committed to a mental facility for treatment.

Today, Scraps gave me a call. Said his shrinks are amazed at his progress. They told him his brain is what they call a resilient organ, and it's re-wiring itself and, when he gets out on probation, him and his new brain are gonna go back and play for the *Clowntown Clowns*.

I just finished a novel about my experience.

Have high hopes for its success.

CPSIA information can be obtained
at www.ICGtesting.com
Printed in the USA
BVHW031031200619
551533BV00006B/145/P